Blood on
The Rails

NED STONE

LEISURE BOOKS NEW YORK CITY

For my sister Phyllis Roth

A LEISURE BOOK®

OCTOBER 1990

Published by

Dorchester Publishing Co., Inc.
276 Fifth Avenue
New York, NY 10001

Printed in the United States of America.

CHAPTER ONE

Other Day Logan had ridden for ten days heading north from Bell's Town looking for a job or some diversion to rid himself of the bad memories he had of the territorial town. Each day seemed to dim the memories and the ache he held in his heart for the loss of Belle Doolin, which was slowly lessening and settling into its place in his mind. She was gone—forever. He didn't think he'd ever meet another woman like her. He had known her for only a few days, but she had made an indelible mark on him, one he thought he'd never lose.

He kept a constant surveillance as he rode the bay gelding toward the northern horizon. He had come far. As best as he could calculate, he had travelled close to 400 miles in the last ten days. He had taken it easy on the horse, covering large pieces of territory at a walk. He'd averaged about 40 miles a day.

He hadn't run into anyone during that time, because he shied away from the few pockets of civilization he had seen. The land had changed dramatically from the dry, almost arid, climate of Bell's Town and the surrounding territory to a gently rolling landscape of rich, lush grass land. He'd seen from a distance several huge herds of cattle but had made a particular effort to avoid the cowboys herding them. The half-breed had wanted to avoid all contact with other human beings while he mourned. And that period seemed to be almost over. He was looking forward to the next day and the next without the anxiety he had had at first. Belle was gone, murdered, and he had killed the men responsible. That was as equal as he could make it. Beyond mourning for the woman, he felt his own life was the only concern he had now.

Suddenly Logan's body began itching. Was danger close by? He cursed the sensation for the inaccurate and inconsistent way it worked for him. Sometimes he understood the warning and sometimes he didn't. He turned in the saddle, scanning the countryside. He could see nothing, no sign of trouble for him. Why, then was he feeling the warning that usually meant danger?

Convinced that the sensation was wrong, he chose to keep riding. But still the sensation persisted.

Other Day guided the bay up a saddleback and stopped before he reached the crest. Listening carefully, he frowned. He could hear voices. Voices were coming over the hill toward the 'breed. He slid off the gelding, ground-tied it, and continued on foot, dropping to his belly before his head cleared the hill's horizon. He inched his way forward until he could see over the lip.

What appeared to be a crew of about 20 men who had been working on some sort of digging project sat on a mound of earth listening to a huge man talking to them. From where he was, Other Day couldn't make out what was being said, but the looks on the faces of the men seemed to indicate they were listening out of fear and not because they wanted to. Each of the seated men was unarmed, but two rifles lay at the foot of the speaker, who was armed.

Logan turned and looked to his right. The work the men had been performing stretched into the distance. They were building the roadbed for a railroad. Well, he could use a drink of water; and since he had found none, he might just as well ask those men for some and then get on with his aimless riding. Turning, he made his way back to his horse and climbed on.

When he rode across the top of the hill, he could feel the eyes of the men below him turning to look at him. Since he was still talking, the big man didn't see Other Day until he was almost on top of him.

"Who the hell are you?" the big man asked, his voice bellowing the question while he drew his gun.

"Who are you?" Other Day shot back.

"None of your business. Get out of here! You got no business around these men." He waved the six-gun in a menacing way.

"All I want is a little water for me and my horse."

"Ain't none here for you. Now git!"

"Give him some water," one of the men said.

"You mighta been the foreman before," the big man snapped, "but I'm here now. I'm giving the orders around here, my fine fellow. I say he gets no water and you men ain't working any more. Understand." He slipped the .45 back into its holster.

"You got no right comin' in here and keepin' us from workin'," one of the seated men said.

The large man strode over to the one who had spoken up and backhanded him across the face. "I got all the right in the world," he snarled over the fallen man.

Other Day slowly dismounted.

"You!" the man shouted. "Get back on your nag and get outta here. You having trouble understan—" The big man stared at Logan. "What in hell are you? A half-breed?"

Other Day walked up to him, his eyes on line with the man's chin. "What if I am. What can you do about it? Make me full-blooded one way or the other?"

"Why you— Don't you get smart with me." He reared back and struck out to hit Other Day, but the breed's knee came up, catching him in the groin.

The man stopped in mid-action, a startled look on his face. Before he could react more, Other Day lashed out with his own fist, catching the man flush on the jaw. The giant fell backward and crashed to the ground.

The men cheered and quickly gathered around their new champion.

"Thanks, stranger," the man who had been backhanded said coming up to Other Day.

"What's wrong with you men. This man is only one and there are twenty of you. Why didn't you jump him?" Other Day's eyes ran over the faces of the men. He had answered his own question when he saw that these were ordinary laborers and not barroom brawlers like the man he had dispatched.

"We think he's a hired gun sent here by the U.L. & B.T. people to stop our work."

Other Day nodded, understanding the situation. "What's the U.L. & B.T. people?" he asked, his curiosity aroused.

"Upper LaMotte and Ball Town Railroad. They got aced out of the contract to build to Hades when the L. A. & H. got the bid. Now, the contract is almost expired, and we have to get a train into Hades within the next ten days or we lose out."

"What's the L. A. & H.?" Other Day asked.

"The Lorraine, Ashton and Hades Railroad.

They're towns along the mainline of this here narrow gauge line. When we reach Hades—if we reach Hades—we get a hundred-thousand-dollar bond grant to continue business. But the U.L. & B.T. or somebody keeps buttin' in, hamperin' us and keepin' us from workin'. By the way, I'm Reinhold Riggs, but everybody calls me 'Hold' for short. Who are you?"

"Name's Logan. What do you want to do with this?" The 'breed nodded toward the unconscious man.

Riggs shrugged. "Tie him up or he'll raise hell once he comes to."

"Why not turn him over to the law?"

"Won't do no good. As far as we know, we think the marshal for the territory is on the U.L. & B.T.'s side. He'd be outta the pokey before you got him in."

Other Day looked around and saw a horse tied to the rear of a supply wagon. A team of mules that had pulled the wagon were hobbled and grazing a short distance away. "That his mount?"

Riggs nodded.

"Have a couple of your men load him on his horse."

Once the large man was belly down across the saddle, Other Day took a length of rope he had found on the rear of the wagon and tied the troublemaker's hands. After throwing the rope under the horse's belly, he walked around to the other side and tied the other end to its feet, making sure the rope was tight.

Slapping the horse on his flanks, Other Day growled and said, "Let him get out of that on his own."

The men laughed and Riggs said, "All right, men, back to work." He turned to Other Day. "Thank you, Mr. Logan. Is there anything I can do for you?"

"I still would like that water for me and my horse. You got any to spare?"

"Sure have, but not for the horse. Our team's already had theirs. Got nothin' but people water in a barrel on the other side of the wagon. Help yourself."

After he filled his canteen, he returned to the foreman. "That's right thoughtful of you to let me have some. I'm beholding to you."

"Other way around," Riggs said. "We're the ones who're beholdin' to you."

The 'breed turned and looked at the grade the men were working on. "Somehow I don't think you're building that quite wide enough. Are you?"

Riggs laughed. "It's not a standard-gauge line we're buildin'. It's narrow-gauge. Only three feet between the rails."

"How come you're building it that way?"

"The folks along the mainline hope it'll be widened to standard gauge in a few years, once they prove there's a lot of business along the mainline."

"Why not build it that way in the first place?"

"Too costly. Maybe a big railroad company will buy it up once it's proven itself."

"I wish the rails were here. I've never seen a narrow gauge train before," Other Day said, thinking back to the regular line that had run into Bell's Town. He'd not had time to see up close one of the railroad locomotives. He found them fascinating and would have taken time to see the one he'd heard when he was there the last time, but he had been too busy.

"End of the track ain't that far away, Mr. Logan. Three miles due east," Riggs said, nodding in that direction. "Just follow the roadbed and you'll come to the end of the track before you know it."

Other Day frowned for a moment, then smiled in his own noncommital way. "Thanks. I'm in no hurry and I just might do that. Thanks again for the water and directions."

"Thank you for stepping in and taking care of that bully. None of us were capable of doing that once he got the drop on us, even if we had him outnumbered."

Other Day saluted him, touching the rim of his Stetson, and then mounted the gelding. He figured that riding a few miles out of the way wouldn't bother him. He had no place in particular to go, and east was just as good a direction to ride in as north.

"I hate to impose on you," Riggs said, "but could you deliver somethin' to the super-intendent if you're intendin' to ride to the end of the track?"

"Depends. What?"

"Just a note."

"Sure. Where is it?"

"It'll only take me a minute to write it out. Can you wait?"

The 'breed nodded and Riggs ran to the wagon. In a moment he returned and handed Other Day a folded piece of paper. "Here you are. Tell Mister Balland to give you a meal for doing this. I'm sure he'll be happy to do so." The foreman smiled as if he had a secret.

Other Day nodded again. He wouldn't turn down a meal if it was a good one. Otherwise, he'd just as soon live off the land the way he'd been doing for the last ten days. "I'm obliged, Mister Riggs," he said and turned the bay's head east to follow the roadbed.

After he had gone a mile, he stopped and got off. Pouring some of the water into his Stetson, he gave the gelding a drink before satisfying his own thirst. He adjusted the Indian headband he wore before putting on the Stetson. Continuing, he soon rode through a cut in a hill and right into the building activity at the track's end.

Men worked without noticing him, and he could see a steam engine in the distance pushing a string of flat cars loaded with rail. Clucking to the bay, he rode toward the locomotive.

The small engine pushed its load ahead a bit at a time, and Other Day wished he could see it running normally rather than just a little every now and then. But the men had to take the rail off, which couldn't be hurried.

When the engine passed, he saw the passenger car hooked on the rear of the work train.

"Hey, there," the 'breed called to a man walking by with a sledge on his shoulder.

"What?"

"Where can I find the big boss? In there?" He pointed to the passenger car.

"If he ain't in there, he's around someplace. Just look for a guy all dressed up. That's him."

Other Day rode up to the rear of the car and jumped onto the platform. After tying the bay to the rear, he stepped up and knocked on the door. It opened and a tall, thin man faced him.

"What can I do for you?"

"Man by the name of Riggs gave me this to give to you if you're Mister Balland," Logan answered.

"I'm Henry Balland," he said, taking the proffered note. "Come in, ah, what was your name?"

"Logan. Other Day Logan."

"Strange name to say the least," Balland said, looking at his guest in an inquisitive way.

Other Day explained how there had been a mix-up at his baptism and how he had never wanted to change it after it had been entered in the church's records as Other Day Logan.

"Sit down, ah, Other Day."

The 'breed lowered himself into a straight back chair, squirming to find a comfortable position.

"Well, this is interesting," Balland said.

Other Day moved to get up.

"No, stay sitting. It seems you saved the day for the grading crew. Took out Bull Turner all by yourself, huh? Reinhold suggests I give you a job as troubleshooter. Would you be interested?"

Other Day looked up. "Troubleshooter? What does a troubleshooter do?" He narrowed his eyes, studying Balland.

"Just what you did to keep Bull Turner from interfering with the construction of this railroad. There've been many attempts by the U.L. & B.T. people to stop us before we get to Hades. At least we think it's the U.L. & B.T. If they do stop us, they can step in and finish the track into Hades and pick up the bonus of a hundred-thousand dollars guaranteed by bonds, to the first company to put a train into Hades."

"That don't hardly seem fair if you people have done all the work to this point. How far is Hades from here?"

"About thirty-five miles."

"How long will it take to get there?"

"It's not a question of how long it will take us to get there, but how much time we have left to get there. We have to be there within ten days or we lose."

Other Day stood up. He didn't want the job. It seemed as if he would be taking on the troubles of this man and his company. The best the 'breed would do was wish them luck. He wanted no part of it.

"Well, sir, I do appreciate your offer. But—"

The door at the end of the coach opened and a young woman stepped inside. Other Day stopped in mid-sentence, unable to speak. It was Belle Doolin. But he had buried her on a hillside south of Bell's Town two weeks earlier.

"Hello, Father," she said nodding to Balland and then glanced at Other Day.

"You were saying, Mr. Logan?"

"Huh? Oh. Yeah! But of course. I'll take the job," he said without taking his eyes off the young woman.

CHAPTER TWO

"Meet Theron Cullen," Henry Balland said, nodding toward Other Day.

The 'breed nodded but didn't offer his hand to the short, squat man.

"Theron," Balland continued, "is our hunter. He provides fresh meat for the crew and handles problems when they come up. However, he found he can't be in two places at once. Is that correct, Theron?"

Theron Cullen eyed the new trouble shooter who stood before him. "You took care of Bull Turner all by yourself?"

Other Day stared back and nodded slowly. He studied the hunter, taking in the knife he wore at his waist and the Winchester rifle he cradled in his left arm. The thing that held his attention longest was the bullwhip, looped over Cullen's left shoulder. Other Day knew something like that could be used as a weapon; and while he had mastered the tools of war and killing of both his mother's people and his father's, he was always interested in adding a new piece to his armament. Maybe this man could teach him how to use such a whip.

"That musta been somethin' to see. I gotta hand it to you if'n you did."

"There's no doubt of that," Henry Balland said, a broad smile on his face. "Since hiring Other Day, I feel as though we might make it into Hades on time now."

"Can you lay thirty-five miles of track in ten days?" Other Day asked.

"If we're not bothered by the U.L. & B.T. guns we can. There's nothing but solid ground between here and Hades. The one trestle we have to cross is almost finished and all we'll have to do when we reach it, is lay the track and continue right on into Hades." Balland looked down at his desk. "Now, if you gentlemen will excuse me, I have some work to do. Theron, you take Other Day around and introduce him to the other foremen. Then take him hunting if you like. But stay within earshot of the end of the track."

Theron nodded and led Logan out of the business car. When they were outside, he turned to the 'breed and said, "I'll bet this is the first time you've ever been paid to help someone go to 'hell.' Am I right?"

Other Day smiled and nodded. He decided he could like Theron Cullen, having detected a certain childlike quality in the fifty-year-old man. "Could you show me how to use that whip?"

"My friend here?" Theron asked, slipping the long, snakelike whip from his shoulder.

"Your friend?" Other Day arched his eyebrows.

"You bet. It's saved my hide a couple of times when usin' a gun wouldn't've been smart or when I couldn't use one."

"How do you mean?"

"Just last week, I was huntin' north o' here in some hilly bluff country and come face to face with a grizzly. My rifle jammed just when I was gonna let him have it. The damned grizz heard the gun click and come chargin' right at me. Ever have a grizz charge at you?"

Other Day shook his head.

"Well, sir, I know'd that bear wasn't about to let me unjam my Winchester, so I dropped it and took the whip. I stood there, waitin' for him to come to me, and when he did, I reared back and popped him right in the nose. The tip of a bullwhacker like this can move pretty darn fast. Dunno how fast, but when you pop it just right it can slice hell outta whatever you wanna cut up. Well, sir, that grizz stopped dead in his tracks, pretty surprised that somethin' had stung him right on the beezer. Before he could get his fightin' wits back together, I let him have it again and again, each time in a new place. By the time I cracked him twenty or thirty times, he was about ready to back down." Theron stopped dramatically and waited for the right moment to continue.

Other Day couldn't wait. "What happened?"

"Some fella from the railroad was comin' toward where me and the bear was havin' our differences of opinion. He told me later he thought a gun fight was goin' on because the whip was crackin' so loud and often."

"I know a popping whip can be heard for over a mile," Other Day said.

"Well, at any rate, the railroad man shot the bear and put the poor thing out of its misery."

"What would have happened if he hadn't come across you and the bear?"

"Believe me, I had the bear goin' and I probably coulda whipped him to death. A body can do that with one of these." He patted the black whip. "You a man o' violence?"

"Only if I have to be, Theron. I prefer peace. I don't start fights, but I usually finish them if someone else gets me into one."

"Come on," Theron said. "I can show you some of the ways to use a whip out in the wilds once we get our meat for the day."

By midday they had shot and killed enough game to last the next day and delivered it to the rail camp. Theron had taken the time to show Other Day how to use the bullwhip and finished by telling the 'breed that it would take practice and more practice to become as efficient with the weapon as he was.

BLOOD ON THE RAILS

That afternoon Other Day and the hunter rode toward the end of the grading work to see how the progress was coming. To the half-breed it seemed an awful long distance to lay something as permanent as railroad tracks in so short a time. Still, Henry Balland seemed to know what he was doing. The grading crew had moved on ahead building the earthen platform on which the ties, rails, and ballast would rest.

When they reached the top of a small rise, Other Day reined to a stop and Theron did the same. Below them in the flat valley, they could see the line of work proceeding. To their left, in the distance, they could make out the grading being done by the ant-sized workers. Closer in, they found the engineer-surveyor leveling ties as they were set in place by men handling the lengths of rough cut timber after they were dropped from a mule-drawn flatbed wagon. Mulewhackers driving three teams brought an unending flow of ties to the proper place. Behind the tie-laying crew, several teams of five ironmen each handled the lengths of rail as they were brought forward on four-wheeled iron trucks. Once the trucks were emptied, they were dumped to the side of the track and replaced on the rails later to bring more rails to the work site. Headspikers set the rails in proper width using a gauge to make certain the two rails were a constant width apart before driving in the spikes.

Horsemen astride single animals towed the

iron trucks along the rails after they were unloaded from flatcars that were pushed ahead by the locomotive. The work train was pulled along behind the narrow gauge engine. That train was home to the workers and moved right along with the progress made on the building of the line.

Other Day watched with mild amusement as some of the men leaned on their shovel handles prying up the rails enough to force the rock-ballast into place. They seemed to be doing a strange dance without touching their feet on the ground in most instances.

"Quite a sight. Isn't it, Theron?" Other Day made a sweeping motion with his arm.

"Yeah, I suppose so. But men like me don't like too many people around. You know what I mean?"

Other Day nodded. "I know exactly what you mean. I'd just as soon not be around too many people at any one time. It makes me sort of nervous."

"You got that right. How come you took the job then?"

Other Day turned away. He couldn't tell Theron that he'd merely agreed to be the troubleshooter to be around Melanie Balland because she reminded him of Belle Doolin. "I guess I thought I could use the money."

"Sad ain't it that two men like you 'n' me have to rely on civilization to get enough money to provide the stuff we need so's we can be alone if'n we want. Why don't we just take off and go into the Rocky Mountains and get ourselves lost? We wouldn't be beholdin' to civilization for nothin' that way."

Other Day smiled ironically. He'd like that. But he'd prefer doing it alone. Maybe that would be what he'd do. If he did, he could ponder on Belle all he wanted and not have to worry about anyone seeing him pine away. "You make it sound like a good idea, but I think I'd better finish this job first. Want to show me more about the whip?"

"Sure, why not. We can keep our eyes and ears open up here just as easily as down there."

Two hours later, Other Day was able to pick a leaf off a tree and wrap the snake-like whip around an arm-sized branch and pull it off. While not as accurate nor consistent as Theron, Other Day felt he could master the whip in time.

When they rode back to the train about a half-mile away, Other Day began feeling uneasy. His body itched a little, and he shifted in his saddle to take in the surrounding countryside. He could see nothing. Was someone out there watching the progress being made on the railroad? Since he had assumed the duty of troubleshooter, he felt obligated to heed any warning he might see or feel. If his erratic warning sense was telling him to be on guard, it was best to take into consideration the welfare of the company at the same time.

When he reached the end of the train, he climbed aboard the business car and went inside.

"Mr. Balland, I think we should consider posting guards along the track at night."

Balland stared at Other Day but said nothing.

Other Day, in turn, studied the tall, distinguished looking man. An expression of relief passed over his face. Whatever it was Other Day felt, he wouldn't have to push the construction superintendent to the extreme and tell him about his warning senses being alerted to possible trouble.

"Under the circumstances, I think it would be a wise precaution," the 'breed said. "We can have some of the men take turns riding the mainline from the camp to the edge of the grading site all night long. I could go to one of the neighboring towns tomorrow and hire new guards to take over tomorrow night."

Balland held up his hand. "I'm not certain I can afford more men on the payroll, Other Day."

"Well, then, I'll ask the men to volunteer to ride two hours at a time. If they have to give up two hours sleep for one night in three or four, no one would be overtaxed in that respect. At least we could feel relatively safe that the work and equipment are being protected."

Pursing his lips, Balland slowly nodded. "We should have been doing that since the trouble with the U.L. & B.T. began. I'll announce it during the evening meal. We'll have most of the men there together at one time."

"If it's all right with you, I'll send Theron out

to the trestle to guard it tonight."

"Yes, by all means. That trestle will prove to be the deciding factor in us getting to Hades on time. It's already completed and waiting for the track to arrive."

"From what I've been able to gather, it sounded pretty important. Maybe we should have men posted there during the daylight hours as well."

"It's extremely important. It crosses a deep ravine and that gulley could keep us from making it into Hades on time if something happens to the trestle. The landscape is really peculiar there. There's a steep bluff to the right of the ravine. In fact the ravine itself, starts right at the base of that hillside. We built the trestle close to that bluff because it was the only logical approach to the gulley itself and provides the narrowest crossing."

"You're saying that if something happened to the trestle, it couldn't be rebuilt in time?"

"Exactly."

Other Day turned to leave and stopped at the door of the business car. "I think I'll send Theron on out there right now."

"I'm glad you came up with this idea, Other Day. We can't afford to take chances."

Other Day nodded and went to find Theron. He felt it would be wise to keep alert himself that night. He'd make the rounds of the camp on a regular basis. The next day he might take the time to ride out and see for himself the trestle Henry Balland had described to him.

As he walked away from the business car, he noticed his itching sensation had quieted considerably. Maybe the posting of guards would be the tonic needed to keep the railroad project moving ahead on time. He hoped so. He wanted no trouble with anyone. Once the rails reached Hades, he'd take his pay and leave to continue his wanderings.

A rare chuckle escaped him when he thought of the fact that he was helping build a railroad to Hades.

CHAPTER
THREE

Other Day reined the bay to a halt and studied the hillside studded with rock outcroppings, which rose above the completed trestle spanning the hundred-twenty-foot ravine. Timber had been cut and hauled to the site from a stand of trees some miles to the north, then trimmed and installed to form a spider-web-like bridge that crossed the gorge.

Clucking to the gelding, he rode forward and approached the structure. The lay of the land was just as Balland had said it was. The split in the surface of the otherwise level landscape widened as it spread to the south. Hilly knolls dotted the countryside, and when he turned in his saddle, Logan saw there was but one reasonable approach to the gulley and that came directly at the spot where the trestle had been built.

When he was at the lip of the ravine, he looked down. It was peculiar how the gorge started at the base of the steep hillside and spread southward. What had caused that to happen? Peering down to the bottom he could see that it was maybe 100 feet or so deep. Not that big of an obstacle for a railroad to overcome as he knew. He'd seen a trestle bridge that was over 1,000 feet long south of Bell's Town and it went right across a valley. This was nothing compared to that bridge, but he could see that given the time element and distance the rails had to go in order to reach Hades, the trestle here, as small as it was, was mighty important to the welfare of the L.A. & H.'s overall plan.

He looked up and saw there were several places where guards could be posted and be protected themselves at the same time. From what he had learned from Balland and Theron, there had been no killings thus far. There had been potshots taken at workers at random, but they never came close enough to anyone to do more than unnerve the men. On some occasions when the work train was backing toward the supply depot that had been established 15 miles to the east, only the sharpest outlook had spotted torn up track and road bed. Hinderances like that—a derailment, a slow-down on work because men were concerned for their safety and troublemakers like Bull

BLOOD ON THE RAILS

Turner arriving to hold up work—could eventually spell doom for the narrow-gauge railroad. If that happened, then the U.L. & B.T. would take over, lay the necessary track into the town and pick up the hundred-thousand-dollar bond grant.

That particular thought irked Other Day. It was dirty and sneaky and the sort of maneuver that would set him off if anyone ever tried it to him. He liked Henry Balland. He seemed a quiet, gentle man and almost unable to cope with the idea of someone being adverse to his plans.

Other Day stopped. Then, too, there was Mr. Balland's daughter Melanie. But the 'breed had barely mumbled a hello to her, and she had virtually ignored him every time they happened to see each other. Her resemblance to Belle was startling. He shook his head. He couldn't think about her like that.

Doing his best to change his thought pattern, he studied the hillside again. He'd have guards posted here day and night with the idea of retreating to the natural hiding spots in the event someone who didn't belong there came around. He had told Theron he could leave at sunup, at which time he rode to the bridge himself. The man he had selected for the day guard was going to follow him after breakfast.

Now that he had the lay of the land in his mind, he wanted to go talk with Henry Balland and discuss another idea he had.

While making the ride back to end of track,

he went over the basic rudiments that Theron had taught him about the bull-whip. On his way to the trestle, he had run into Theron, who had stood guard at the trestle the previous night. They had talked for a moment, and then the hunter continued on toward the north while Other Day went on his way to the trestle. He thought about the short squat man for a moment. He definitely found likeable qualities in Theron Cullen, and the fact that he was willing to teach Other Day about the bullwhip made him seem even nicer in the eyes of the 'breed. He seldom made close ties to anyone, but he felt that he and Theron could form some sort of friendship that both men could understand and not look on as a hinderance to each of their individual spirits.

When he rode into camp, he went immediately to the business car and found Henry Balland hunched over his desk. The superintendent looked up when the 'breed entered.

"Good morning," he said, his manner and voice reflecting the relief that he could stop working for a few minutes. "What can I do for you?"

"Did you make your three and a half miles yesterday?"

"We fell short about two-hundred yards, which isn't too bad, and we can surely make that up over the next few days. Why?"

"Well, you're cutting it thin. And if something were to happen that would cause you to fall even further behind, you wouldn't have the time to make it up, would you?"

Balland stood and walked around his desk. "Unfortunately, you're right. I don't know what I'd do if something underhanded was done by the U.L. & B.T."

"I got another idea."

"What's that? If it's as good as the posting of guards, I'm for it."

"Where does this gang hang out? Do you know?"

"If it is the U.L. & B.T., their headquarters would be in Ball Town. That's about fifteen miles south and east of here. Why?"

"They don't know me and I might be able to find something out if I went there. I can be back after dark tonight and let you know if I learned anything."

Balland sucked on his empty pipe, then blew hard through it. "I don't know." He reached in his pocket and pulled out a pouch of tobacco. Carefully tamping his pipe, he seemed to ignore Other Day while he pondered the idea.

The 'breed waited.

"You be careful, Other Day. I wouldn't want anything to happen to you because of me and my railroad."

"I don't like the idea of getting into trouble, either, Mr. Balland, but I can take care of myself." He turned and walked to the rear of the car and leaped into the saddle on the bay who was tied to the platform. Just as he wheeled the gelding to ride south, he saw

Melanie Balland walking along the side of the business car. He stared for a long minute, marveling at her resemblance to Belle Doolin. A lump formed in his throat and he turned away, spurring the bay into a gallop to get away from the camp.

As he rode, he thought about the Balland woman. She was a dead ringer for Belle—or as close as two people could look alike—and that wasn't good. He had found himself uncovering the almost healed wounds caused by Belle's death when thinking about Melanie Balland. That wasn't right. He could not allow himself to become involved with her on any basis. It wouldn't be fair to her nor would it be fair to him. The ghost of Belle Doolin would always hover between them no matter how hard they tried to ignore the—

"Shut up your crazy thoughts, half-breed," he yelled aloud.

He was fantasizing and that wasn't like him. More than likely Melanie Balland would have nothing to do with him anyway. She appeared to be a cultured and educated young lady, and he was nothing but a man with two different types of blood flowing through his veins. He had nothing to offer a woman like her.

To get the phenomenon of the close resemblance off his mind, he began practicing cracking an imaginary whip as Theron Cullen had shown him. Theron had told him he would be able to crack a whip when he could snap his wrist hard enough and let his fingers loose enough to snap loudly themselves. After 20 minutes of practice, he heard his fingers make the sound and he smiled broadly.

After two more hours of slow riding, he entered Ball Town. It wasn't his nature to be falsely friendly to anyone. So he decided rather than trying to strike up a conversation with someone to learn information he'd go to the saloon owned by Asa Horton, the president of the U.L. & B.T.. Balland had told him about Horton and the Gilded Garter in Ball Town and how that was where Horton's gang hung out.

He tied the bay gelding to the hitching rail in front of the saloon and entered. In a way it reminded him of the Gold Nugget in Bell's Town. It was one room with a staircase leading to the second floor, where a fallen angel's attentions and affections could be had for a price. Several doors opened onto the other rooms at the rear and on one side of the main floor. He assumed that one was an office and the others storerooms or something along that line. He didn't care because he had no plans on staying around Ball Town. He'd find out whatever he could that would be of use to Balland and then clear out. He only hoped he could learn something.

Making his way to the bar, Other Day noted that a group of men were seated at a table in one corner and that they weren't playing cards. One or two had their heads down on the table itself, and two more were sitting upright, sound asleep.

"What do you need, stranger?" the bartender asked.

"Whiskey and a beer." After giving his order, Other Day turned and looked around the room again. Two men were huddled close together in conversation to his right. When he heard the bartender set the glasses on the bar behind him, he turned around and fixed his attention on the whiskey and beer, but tuned his hearing in on the two men to his side.

"It's tomorrow?" one asked.

"Yup. Thet's what the boss said."

"And he's knocking out the bridge?"

"Yup. Dynamitin' it to kingdom come. Thet'll stop 'em, by God!"

They laughed and Other Day did his best not to react.

When the men stopped laughing, one said, " 'Course that's the straw what'll break Balland's back. There's no way he can rebuild it and get into Hades on time when thet happens."

Other Day lifted the beer to his lips and stopped. His body itched. Something was going to happen. He felt certain. The sensation was horrible. He wanted to scratch and jump around to ease the discomfort, but he knew he couldn't. But what was going to happen? He'd have to wait and see. Grabbing the shot glass of whiskey, he threw it down. The burning in his throat helped take his mind away from the other feeling.

Then the door swung open and he heard a

deep, hearty laugh from behind. "Well, my fine fellows, you look like you're all bored to death. Let's play us some cards."

Other Day didn't move. He knew the voice and the expression 'fine fellows.' It was the man he'd dispatched at the grading site the day before. How had he gotten off his horse? Perhaps the animal had turned and brought the man back to Ball Town, homing in on his stall and oats. No matter what happened, Other Day knew he was in trouble. He hadn't counted on Bull Turner showing up.

"Been out riding your horse belly down and cross-saddle?" one of the man at the table asked.

"That's not a very friendly thing to say, my friend. You aren't makin' fun of me, are you?"

Other Day heard a chair scrape on the floor and then fall back to the floor itself.

"No, Bull. No. I wasn't makin' no fun of you. I'd never do that. You know that."

"Well," Bull said, bending down to pick up the fallen chair, "it wasn't a nice thing for that goddamned half-breed to do. I assume it was him, after kickin' me in my privates like he done. I tell you men right now if'n I ever find him I'll enjoy beating him. I take that from no man. No sir."

Other Day played with the glass of beer. He could turn, challenge Bull Turner to gunplay, and probably outdraw him. But that would mean he'd be held here in Ball Town and not be able to leave to report back to Henry Balland to warn him of what he'd learned. He'd have to hope he could leave the saloon unnoticed by Bull Turner.

"Say, Bull," one of the men said and whispered conspiratorially to the huge man across the table.

Other Day strained his own hearing but couldn't pick up what was being said. At least 15 feet separated him from the table. He hoped it was nothing and the men would become engrossed in a game of cards.

"Where?" Bull asked.

"At the bar," the first speaker said.

Other Day could hear a chair being shifted, and he felt his body going out of control with the itching. Maybe he should just draw and—

"You. At the bar. Turn around. My man here says you're a half-breed. Are you?"

"Me no savvy," Other Day said haltingly.

"Then how did you know I was talkin' to you. Turn around." Bull's voice rumbled the words loudly.

Other Day heard a hammer being cocked and then several more. His luck had run out. He had to face them or run the risk of being gunned down from behind. Slowly, he came around, his hands in sight, but not so far that he couldn't make a last desperate move for his .44.

"Well, now look who's here," Bull said, standing up and kicking a chair and table that separated him from the bar out of his way. "Howdy, half-breed."

Other Day said nothing, his eyes scanning the seven men standing before him.

Bull walked up to him. "You're right quick with your knee, half-breed. What say we settle our differences in a manly way."

"I'm no fool, Bull."

"Oh, you know my name, do you?"

"I know who you are. But I won't fight you with six guns held on me."

"Is that what's botherin' you, my fine fellow? Boys, put the guns away. This is between me and the half-breed here. If he wins, take care of him."

"Not much point in my trying to win or even fight is there, Bull?" the 'breed said evenly.

Bull frowned, trying to understand what the 'breed had said. Rather than try to figure it out, he folded his huge, ham-like hand into a ball and struck out at Other Day. The 'breed ducked to one side and brought his own fist up to strike Bull on the jaw. The blow was deflected and he struck the huge man in the throat, cutting off his breath for a moment.

Following up his advantage, Other Day moved in ready to strike the huge man again. The six men fell to the sides and suddenly Other Day felt his own arms being held. Two men had grabbed him, holding him tightly. A third grabbed the 'breed's .44, disarming him.

Bull held his throat and coughed. When the spasm passed, he glared at Other Day. "I hate men who fight dirty, and you fight dirty by my book, half-breed. Now, I'm going to teach you a lesson."

"Having two men hold me isn't fighting dirty, you big—"

Other Day's words were cut short when Bull struck him across the face. The 'breed's head popped to one side. Another blow threw it back in the other direction. His head swam and lights sparkled in his blurred vision. When Bull punched him in the stomach, he doubled over as far as he could in the grips of the men holding him. His breath whooshed out and he gasped, fighting for air.

From a far off distance, he heard Bull roar, "Let him go, boys, he's mine now."

When his arms were free, Other Day sank to the floor. Then he felt the toe of Bull's boot crash into his lower chest and stomach. He gagged, his stomach heaving desperately trying to throw up what he had long ago eaten.

Then a new voice cut through the darkening veil falling across Other Day's eyes.

"Stop it, Bull. Not here. Who is that?"

"The half-breed what tied me to my horse when I was out convincin' the graders to stop diggin'."

"Does he work for the L.A. & H?"

"He must. He wouldn't have done to me what he done 'lessen he worked for 'em."

"Well, if he's a L.A. & H. man throw him in the small cellar with the stuff out back. We can't let him go back to their camp and tell them what happened here. They may suspect us, but they have no proof that it's been us tryin' to stop 'em from gettin' into Hades. Hurry up and do that. Then come to my office. I'm goin' to lay out the final plans.''

Semiconscious, Other Day felt himself being half-carried, half-dragged along the floor and through a doorway. His feet bounced on steps as they went outside. After what seemed an eternity, he thought they entered another building. In seconds, he was being dragged down more steps and into a darkened cellar. When they reached the bottom, his captors threw him into another room, which was much smaller than the cellar itself. He heard a door close and something click into place.

His mind flashed off and on for a long moment while he tried to lift himself, and then he fell down on the earthen floor and sank into the deep, black morass of unconsciousness.

CHAPTER
FOUR

The 'breed moaned and rolled onto his side.

Other Day stood perfectly still, facing down the man confronting him. He stared at the white hair and the half ear that were exposed. He hated this man. He wanted to kill him in the worst way imaginable.

The man with the half ear opened his mouth. His voice sounded strange—too deep, too slow. What was wrong with him? Other Day strained his hearing to understand what the man was trying to say.

"I killed your mother, you ignorant half-breed son of a bitch! Now I'm goin' to mark you for life."

The man took a slow, giant step toward Other Day. Other Day knew he had to do something, but what. He tried to move. He couldn't. Something or someone held him. The man with the long white hair came closer. Other Day shrunk back. He wanted to run, to get away, to hide. But he could not. The man was closer now, almost within arm's reach. He drew his gigantic six-gun and swung it in a slow arc, the barrel tip and sight coming straight at Other Day's face. He turned away, but he couldn't escape the swinging gun barrel. He felt it strike his jaw, sending a shock of pain through his head and body. Before he could move, the man swung again from the opposite direction, ripping his cheek open again. Other Day heard a growling scream coming from somewhere and was startled to hear the cry coming from deep within himself. For a third time, the man swung the pistol, striking Other Day across the same cheek, tearing it open even farther.

The 'breed could feel warm blood running down his face. He screamed again and then yelled, "I'll kill you, you dirty white bastard! I'll kill you with my bare hands, damn you!"

He felt sick to his stomach and gagged when bile rose in his throat.

He moaned and opened his eyes. He couldn't see anything. Where was he? His head felt awful. What had happened? He'd been in a bar and someone—*Bull Turner!* Bull Turner had beaten him up while two of his men held him by the arms and he couldn't defend himself.

Other Day rolled over onto his back and stared into the blackness. Where the hell was he? Where had they put him? He tried sitting up and found his head throbbed even more when he moved it. But he had to get up. Even in the dark, he felt more vulnerable lying on his back than if he were sitting up or standing.

He lay back and rested for a moment. If he gave it time, his head might clear sufficiently to allow him to move without the dizzying sensation. He replayed the dream he'd had for a moment. That had not bothered him for many years. Sure, he'd searched out and finally found the man who had murdered his mother and had exacted the pound of flesh he felt due him. Pound of flesh, hell. He'd maimed the man by cutting off half of his good ear to give him a matched pair. Then, so he'd have a reminder of what Other Day Logan had done in retaliation for the death of his mother, he'd shot the man in both knees. He wanted the bastard to remember him every time he tried to walk. At first he'd thought of scalping the sonofabitch, but had decided against it, cursing the white blood flowing through his veins that had stopped him from doing what the Indian half wanted. Still, he had left a knife cut along the man's hair line just to let him know how damned lucky he was that the Pawnee blood hadn't won out.

Other Day wondered what had prompted the dream? Maybe the fact that two men held him while Bull Turner beat him up. Who knew? Who cared? All he cared about at the moment was getting mobile enough to examine the room he was in and finding a way out. He'd tend to Bull Turner later.

He tried sitting up again and found his head less dizzy. Instinctively reaching up to his cheek, he felt the z-shaped scar that Half Ear Hantlemann had made when he pistol-whipped him. It was still there. It would always be there. The dream had been so real he felt he might find blood flowing from it.

Reaching around behind his neck he felt for the throwing knife. It was there. They had taken his .44 but hadn't searched him for other weapons. He felt along his leg and found the handle of the Bowie knife in his right boot and the hunting knife in his left.

He drew one leg up and pushed off, coming to a standing position. Swaying for a moment, he reached out for something to steady himself with and found a rock wall. His head spun and it was several minutes before he felt secure in his upright position. Once the dizziness and unsteadiness left him, he could feel his strength returning. Running his fingers over the wall, he decided he must be in some sort of cellar. He inhaled deeply and found the air damp and stale. Then he smelled something else, but couldn't put a finger on it to identify it.

He reached in his pocket and found three stick matches. He struck one on the rock wall and shielded it with his hand, holding it up to get as much illumination as possible.

The room was small, no more than ten feet by ten. And there were boxes stacked along the wall. He moved closer and stopped, freezing in his tracks. *Dynamite!* He quickly counted the cases. 36 boxes of dynamite. More than enough to blow him and the town of Ball Town out of existence. He stayed where he was, not moving closer to the store of explosives. From where he stood, he could see there were no windows and only one door, the one they apparently brought him through. He looked overhead and found beams and a floor. The only way out was through the door.

The match went out. He moved to the door and lighted another match. He quickly examined the hinges and found they were on the outside. He pushed on the heavy door and it moved an inch or so. Bending down, he peered through the crack between the door and the jamb. The match died when he bent down and he pulled the last one out.

After lighting it, he peered through the crack again and found a two-by-four holding the door closed. If there was no lock, and nothing but a latch, he could get out with no problem. Reaching down, he slipped the Bowie knife through the flapped slit in his pants leg and stuck it through the crack. Lifting it, he moved the bar and pushed on the door. It swung open, making a creaking noise. He moved it slowly, hoping no one was around. When it was open far enough, he stepped through and caught sight of a flight of steps leading up just as the last match went out.

Keeping the picture of the steps in his mind,

he moved ahead, making no sound as he did. He reached out with his right foot and found the first riser. He put his foot down close to the end of the step and put his weight on it. No creak. He repeated the process for the next step and the next until he stood at a closed door. Fumbling around, he searched out the doorknob or handle. When he found it, he decided it was a lift-type latch and tried it. It worked and he pushed that open a scant inch. He listened carefully. He could detect no sounds other than night noises.

Night? What time was it? How long had he been out? Was he even in Ball Town anymore?

He swung the door open and stepped into what appeared in the half gloom in which he found himself to be another store room of some sort. Boxes of food stuffs and cases of whiskey were piled to the ceiling.

There was sufficient light for him to see several windows and a door with a window in it off to his left. He stepped toward it without making a sound. He froze when he heard a voice.

"When will Bull and the boys be back?" the voice said.

Other Day pressed against the wall and tried to see who was talking outside.

"Probably by mornin'. If'n you want to go git some grub at the eatery go on. I just et. I can stand guard here 'til you get back." The second man burped after he finished speaking.

"Thet's mighty nice o' you, Red. I'll do it now."

"You heard anythin' outta that half-breed sonofabitch?"

"Not a sound. For all I know Bull killed him with his bare hands when he pounded on him like he done. And it wouldn't be the first time, neither."

"Hurry on back and why don't you bring a bottle along for us to while away the hours."

"Good idea, Red. I'll do it."

Other Day could hear footsteps fading as the first man walked away. Then more footsteps as the man called Red moved toward the building. The 'breed pressed against the wall when the clump of boots sounded on a board porch outside. It couldn't have been better for Other Day. Red was coming to him. He stood perfectly still and waited. The knob turned and the door swung in. Other Day gripped the Bowie knife and waited until the man stepped inside. After the door was closed, Other Day stepped forward and tapped the man on the shoulder. He turned around.

"Yeah?"

Other Day lashed out with the butt of the knife, catching Red in the middle of his forehead. He dropped like a sack of potatoes.

The 'breed stood over him for a moment. It wouldn't do to have the other guard come back and find him like this. Dragging the unconscious man over to the door that led to the basement, he pulled him down the steps and then threw him in the store room that had served as Other Day's prison. Slipping off the man's belt, he bound his hands and then wrapped his handkerchief around his mouth, pulling it tight. Logan ripped off the man's shirt and used it to bind his feet together. Satisfied the man could neither move nor yell out, Other Day left the room and set the latchbar back in place.

He quickly retraced his steps to the upper floor and stepped outside. Where the hell was he? How far from the Gilded Garter had they taken him? In the dim light of a quarter moon, he saw the outlines of buildings in front of him. Was one of them the Gilded Garter? He could hear music playing someplace—a violin and a banjo. It seemed to be coming from straight ahead. Running to the shadows of the largest building in front of him, he pressed against the wall and listened. The music was coming from inside. It was the Gilded Garter. Now what had they done with his horse? He needed that to get the hell out of Ball Town.

Sliding along the wall of the building, he slowly groped along the narrow passageway between the saloon and the building next door. When he reached the street, he waited for a moment to see if anyone who might be opposed to the idea that he was free and running around loose was about. When he heard nothing other than the violin and banjo playing a Virginia reel, he stepped into the street. It was deserted. The only animal he saw was one tied to the rail in front of the Gilded Garter.

He moved closer. It looked like the bay gelding. When he was within 15 feet of the horse, the animal nickered softly. It *was* his gelding. Untying the leather line, he swung into the saddle and walked the horse away from the saloon. Most of the buildings in the small town were already dark, and when he checked the moon again, he found it quite high. It was late. But how late?

When he reached the outer buildings of Ball Town, he urged the bay along at a canter-like gait. He could cover the distance between Ball Town and the end of track camp in three or four hours and not have to worry about running the risk of having the gelding hurt himself in the dark.

His head pounded as he rode through the gloomy night. A chill breeze wound through the air, whipping over him, sending a chill down his back. It was late autumn, and while there had been no hard freeze yet, it could happen most any night. He'd have to take some of the money he would be paid for being the trouble-shooter for the L.A.& H. and get some long underwear if he were going to stay in this part of the country very long.

He took a deep breath and gasped. A pain shot through his lower chest. What was wrong? Why hadn't he felt the pain before? He ran his hand along the bottom of his rib cage on the left side and winced at the sudden discomfort it caused. Had he been so intent on dispatching the guard and escaping that he hadn't noticed it?

Then he remembered Bull Turner kicking him in the chest and stomach when he had been knocked down.

Bull Turner.

Other Day saw red in the dark night. Bull Turner would pay for the pain he had caused the 'breed. Although he had never had a broken rib before, he felt certain he had one now. Bull Turner would have to have a couple of bones broken in return to set the scales even as far as Other Day was concerned. And what about Asa Horton? The man had hired Bull Turner and was trying to take the bond money of a hundred-thousand dollars from L. A. & H. by turning men like Bull loose on the railroad. Well, maybe Other Day Logan hadn't had a stake in the fight other than being troubleshooter before, but now he felt he had a personal stake in the completion of the road.

Less than three hours later, Other Day spotted the end-of the track campfires burning in the distance. Urging the bay on, he rode into the area where one of the guards challenged him.

"Hold it right there, Mister. Up with your hands. Who are you?"

Other Day raised both hands, keeping the reins in his right. "It's me. Other Day Logan."

"Where the hell you been?"

Other Day dropped his hands and started ahead. "Ball Town. Why?"

"We were attacked tonight by some side-winding bandits who stampeded our animals and held us down with rifle fire while some of their men made off with a lot of our dynamite."

Other Day reined to a stop. "What? Where's Mister Balland?"

"Him and most of the men are over by the business car."

Other Day kicked the bay in the sides and galloped ahead. In seconds, he was swinging out of the saddle, unmindful of the pain in his lower chest. "Mr. Balland," he called, pushing his way through the men.

"Other Day?" Balland's eyes widened in the flickering campfire. "My God, man, what happened to you?"

Reactions from the other men swept through the gathering when they looked at the trouble-shooter of the L.A. & H.

"What's the matter?" he asked, startled by their reactions.

"Your face is puffed up and both of your eyes are blackened." Balland stepped closer, turning the half-breed to the light of the nearest campfire. "You'd better have Melanie take a look at that. What happened?"

Other Day told him about his encounter with Bull Turner and his men at the Gilded Garter. When he finished, he said, "What happened here?"

"About three hours ago, a bunch of men started firing at the camp and had us pinned down pretty good before we could get our hands on our rifles and such. The guards were taken by surprise, and while we were shooting back at the men on the south side of us, others were taking the dynamite from the powder car behind us. It was a simple plan but it worked effectively."

"Did they get it all?"

"No. I'd say they got maybe half of it. No more."

"Who were they?" the 'breed asked, unmindful of the pain.

"I don't know. I didn't see anyone of them clearly enough to make out a face. Did any of you men see anyone you might recognize?"

A negative murmur ran through the crowd.

"I'll bet your hundred-thousand dollars that it was Horton's men, led by Bull Turner," Other Day said matter of factly.

"You found something out?" Balland's face brightened.

"I overheard some men talking about it right before I got aced out by Bull. It was them, all right. But I wonder why they wanted to run the risk of stealing your dynamite? I happen to know they've got plenty of their own."

"I have no—"

Balland was cut off by a rumbling from the west.

"What was that?" Balland asked.

"It came from the direction of the trestle. Turner and his men have blown it up," Other Day said, looking west.

CHAPTER
FIVE

Henry Balland stared toward the western horizon. "I'm through. That's it. They've won."

Other Day turned to his employer. He couldn't believe what he'd heard. What was he thinking? Was he willing to give up so easily without even seeing the damage that had apparently been wrought on the trestle? Other Day fought the urge to turn and walk away. He disliked people who were able to give up at the first sign of trouble. Still, he knew that Henry Balland had had more than his share of obstacles to overcome with this railroad. He hadn't given up then. Why was he willing to give up now? Was it too much for him?

"Mr. Balland," Other Day said quietly, "I think it would be a good idea to see first what the damage is and then plot your course of action. Why wave the flag of surrender here and now without knowing?"

Balland continued looking at the western horizon. "Of course, you're right, Other Day. As soon as it's light, we'll go there and assess the damage. Perhaps it isn't as bad as I think it might be."

"That's better. I didn't think you were that sort of a man, Mr. Balland."

"What sort is that?" He turned to face the 'breed.

"From the first time I met you, I thought I saw something in your eyes that set you apart from other men. You've got a sense of determination that I know well."

Balland smiled. "The rest of you men had better get back to sleep. We've got a railroad to build tomorrow. Where's Dismus Scott?"

The engineer-surveyor for the Lorraine, Ashton and Hades Railroad stepped closer to Balland and said, "Right here, Mr. Balland."

"You're riding to the trestle with us in the morning. You're the only one who can accurately tell if the damage is severe enough to wipe us out. Get some rest and we'll call you at dawn."

Scott nodded and turned to leave the superintendent and troubleshooter standing with the hunter. Theron stepped closer to Other Day. "Say, you'd better have them black eyes tended to before we go to the trestle."

"We?" Balland asked.

"Sure. I thought that was long as I'm the full-time hunter and part-time troubleshooter I could sorta do both jobs. I'll ride with you fellers as troubleshooter and then sorta mosey on and do my other job. If'n that's all right with you, Mr. Balland, sir." Theron looked at Other Day and winked.

Other Day nodded and reached up to touch his right eye. He blinked at the pain and felt that it was swollen.

Balland caught him touching the eye and said, "I'll have Melanie take a look at those wounds of yours before we go in the morning."

"There's no time for that. She's sleeping right now and I insist that you let her be. If there's time when I get back from the trestle site, I'll think about it and then see how I feel. Actually, I'm in a lot better shape than I should be, considering the walloping I took from Bull Turner."

"Very well," Balland said. "I'll see you at first light." He turned and walked toward the business car at the end of the work train.

"Nice man but don't know nothin' about black eyes and such," Theron said, spitting on the ground.

"They aren't that bad, Theron." Other Day rubbed his hands over his lower chest. The ribs still hurt him, and he knew it would only delay things if he were to tell anyone about them before they went to the trestle in the morning. If they still hurt when they got back, he might say something. But pain was an old friend of his and he'd spent a lot of time with it. He'd been hurt more severely then this and gone without attention to wounds. The z-shaped scar on his cheek attested to the fact that he could stand pain. Father McGhee had bandaged it when he found Other Day the day after his mother had been murdered; and within an hour after the wound had been wrapped, the 'breed was out trying to find out something concerning the whereabouts of his mother's killer.

"Your ribs ain't in too good a shape, are they?" Theron asked and winked.

Other Day shot a quick, menacing glare at the short, squat man. "Who said anything about ribs?"

"Shucks, you didn't have to say nothin'. I been watchin' you and every time you touch 'em, you make a face. Oh, I'll grant you it ain't much of a pained look you get. But if you're like me, even though they hurt like hell, you wouldn't tell anyone to save your hide. Am I right?"

Other Day turned and walked toward where he and the hunter had bedded down under the stars. While he unsaddled the gelding and hobbled him, he looked up and saw the tiny pin-points of light. They sparkled in the clear, crisp air of the fall night. It wouldn't be long before the first killing freeze. He didn't know if he wanted to hang around that part of the country and be uncomfortable in the snow that would eventually come. He wasn't tied down to any one place or any one person, so he could come and go as he chose. Perhaps he'd go to Texas by way of Oklahoma and see Father McGhee. He hadn't seen the priest in almost five years. He wondered how he was.

Once he managed to lie down, Other Day pulled up the blanket and covered it with a piece of tarpaulin.

"You sleepin' yet, Other Day?" Theron asked.

"No."

"Let me wrap your chest in the mornin' before the boss sees you."

"No."

"Dagnabit, you're such a stubborn cayuse."

"It serves me well in times."

"Yeah, and I'll bet at other times you're as miserable as a polecat. Why, I—"

Other Day faked a snore, and Theron turned over in his own bedroll and went to sleep.

The 'breed smiled and turned his back to the hunter. He liked Theron, and the fact that he had offered to tend Logan's wounds made him think even more of the man. As rough as Theron Cullen was, Other Day Logan knew that beneath that buckskin outfit he wore and the rough, uncouth exterior beat a heart that was as big as a horse's and that was willing to sacrifice anything for someone he liked and respected. Other Day felt, for the first time in a long time, close to another human being.

His ribs still hurt in the morning but he lied to Theron, saying they felt much better. Other Day waited until the hunter had mounted his pinto and turned to ride toward the business car leading his pack mule before he pulled himself into the saddle. He gasped and found that once he was seated in the saddle his ribs stopped hurting him. He wondered what it would be like to ride at a fast pace.

Puffs of steam squirted from the gelding's nostrils and a thin film of white frost clung to the long grass where they had slept. It had frozen a bit but not that much.

He walked the horse to the business car and waited for Balland to make an appearance. Dismus Scott rode up on a nondescript roan mare and said good morning. Other Day acknowledged the engineer's greeting, but said nothing beyond that. As always, he wasn't in the mood for small talk.

While Theron checked over his Winchester rifle and .50 caliber buffalo gun, Other Day reached down to the empty holster where the Smith and Wesson .44 usually hung. Bull Turner or one of his men had Logan's gun. He needed a side arm, but where was he going to find one out here in the wilderness? Sure, he had his three knives and Winchester rifle, but he felt vulnerable without the .44.

Henry Balland stepped out onto the rear platform of the business car and inhaled deeply. "Good morning, men. I trust you slept well, despite the little time you had to sleep. It's cool this morning, isn't it?"

While Scott and Theron nodded their agreement, Other Day walked the bay to the car and looked at Balland. "I need a gun. Bull Turner took mine. Do you have one I could use until I retrieve mine from him?"

"Well, now, I can't have my troubleshooter walking around unarmed. Just a moment." He walked back into the car, returning in a moment with a handgun. "Here, Other Day, use it as long as you need it. In fact, why not keep it as a gift?"

Other Day took the gun and checked it. It was fully loaded and felt well balanced. He looked up. "Thank you, Mr. Balland. It's a nice piece. I've never owned a Colt before, but I appreciate the gift. Thank you again."

Other Day noticed that the superintendent carried a rifle of his own. Balland swung down from the car and walked toward the tether line where he chose a sorrel gelding to ride. After it was saddled, he took the lead and the four men rode toward the trestle.

"Was anyone at the trestle last night on guard duty?" Other Day asked.

"No," Theron said before anyone else could answer. "I had been, but I came into camp to send another man out just about the time the shooting started. Nobody else was sent afterward."

"I was wondering why nobody thought about seeing if any guards might be all shot up out there. There weren't any, huh?" Other Day shook his head in dismay. Of course, if there had been someone on duty, there might have well been a death involved.

The 'breed squirmed in his saddle trying to find a position that wouldn't bother his injured ribs when he and the others started riding faster. He tended to hang back to keep the others from seeing his discomfort. Every once in a while, Theron looked back but didn't say anything.

Winding their way through the small knoll-like hills that dotted the landscape, they made their way toward the trestle. When they reached it, they reined to a stop and dismounted.

"Well, gentlemen," Henry Balland said after a moment's silence during which they perused the pile of timber that had been a trestle, lying at the bottom of the hundred-foot deep ravine, "it's as I feared." He turned and looked at Scott. "Is there any way possible that it might be rebuilt in time?"

Scott shook his head. "Aye, I'm afraid not, Mr. Balland. Even if we had the timber here, which we don't, it would take at least a week to rebuild it—and then only if we had everyone working on it day and night." He fell silent.

Theron spat into the gulley and turned away. Other Day ignored the destroyed bridge and looked around. Then his attention fell on the bluff rising 200 feet over the site.

"Why not fill the ravine up?" he asked.

Scott laughed. "That would take even longer."

"Not if you blew hell out of that bluff there. It's twice as high as the ravine is deep. Couldn't

62

you place dynamite in the right spots and keep blowing it up until it was full?"

Balland stared at Other Day and then turned to Scott. "Well, Dismus? Could it be done?"

Scott studied the bluff for several minutes and then walked to the edge of the ravine. "Aye! Aye, I think it would work. Yes. It will. But do we have enough dynamite to do it?"

Balland shrugged. "I don't know. We'll have to check our inventory and see when we get back." He turned to Other Day. "Great idea, Other Day. I—"

Other Day turned in his saddle to acknowledge Balland. But as he turned, he jarred his sore ribs and sucked in his breath.

"What is it? Are you hurt?" Balland asked.

"It's nothing. I—"

"He's got some banged-up ribs, Mr. Balland. I tried to get him to let me wrap 'em up last night, but before I could even suggest it he turned over and went to sleep." Theron turned to Other Day. "Want I should do it now, 'breed?"

"I—"

"I'll have Melanie check him when we get back to the camp. Mr. Cullen?"

"Yes, sir."

"Are you going hunting from here?"

"Thet's what I sorta planned on doin'. You got other ideas?"

"No. Get going. We're going to finish this road or I'll know the reason why."

Theron spurred the pinto and rode away to

the north, the pack mule trotting along behind.

"Let's get back to camp and check our inventory of blasting powder and dynamite," Balland said and cracked his sorrel on the flanks.

Scott fell in behind him and Other Day shook his head. He'd take his time to ride back. No sense killing himself with pain by galloping. The quick trot they'd managed all the way out had been hard enough on him.

When he rode into camp, he found Balland and Scott talking. Both looked as if they'd just been told the world was going to end that evening.

"What's wrong?" he asked, when he rode up to them.

"We don't have enough powder left," Balland looked up at Other Day with a look of expectation on his face, as if begging Logan to come up with another idea that will save the day.

"Why not ride into Hades and get what you need?"

"We got the last they had. And as far as I know there isn't any at Ashton or Lorraine. Besides, we'd have to blast by tomorrow morning if we're going to win this race with time." Balland took out his handkerchief and wiped his face.

"I know where there's a lot of dynamite. In fact, in a way it belongs to you since the U.L. & B.T.men took yours," Other Day said.

"What?" Balland and Scott chorused.

"At Ball Town. When they locked me up, they

put me in a room with quite a few boxes of dynamite. Why don't we go get it?"

Balland turned away for a moment and then faced Other Day. "How many men would it take to get it?"

"Two—no more than three."

"No. I want to take an army of men. We'll take the workmen. By Godfrey, we'll show them a thing or two." Balland punched a fist into his open palm.

"I don't think that would be too smart."

"And why not?"

"Suppose you get the dynamite and lose half your men doing it? You won't have the man power to finish building the road."

Balland shook his head and sighed. "As usual you're right. What do you propose?"

"I'll take Theron and maybe one other man to drive a team of mules. Two men, like Theron and me, can get into Ball Town and get that dynamite without being seen."

"You know better about that, I suppose." Balland said.

"How much do you need, Mr. Scott?" the 'breed asked.

"With what we have here, I'd say two, three-hundred pounds should do it."

"When Theron gets back, we'll start. It'll take all night to go there by mule wagon and back, once we get the dynamite."

"In the meantime, Mr. Logan, I want you to see you Melanie about your ribs, and I mean *now*."

"I don't suppose—" Other Day started to say.
"I said *now*. She's waiting for you at the
business car. Get going, or I won't approve of
you going tonight and we'll just shut down."

The 'breed shook his head. He didn't understand why Balland acted as if the railroad
belonged to Other Day. Nevertheless, he turned
the bay in the direction of the passenger car
at the end of the work train and rode slowly
toward it.

Other Day felt embarrassed. His shirt was
spread on a table and Melanie Balland hovered
over him with a roll of bandages. She'd
commented on the bullet wound in his left
shoulder, and he'd told her it had been an
accident. Why go into details of having been
shot from behind when his defenses had been
down?

"Maybe it would be best if you stood up, Mr.
Logan."

He did as she suggested. "Why don't you call
me Other Day?"

"All right, Other Day. You can call me
Melanie. Now, take a deep breath and hold it."

He did and she began wrapping the cloth
bandage around his middle, slipping her arms
around his body to continue unraveling the
material.

"How did you get that nasty scar on your
face?" she asked.

He didn't want to tell her the whole story.
How could he without being crude? He turned

away. He couldn't look directly at her. It was as if Belle were there caring for him. "Let's just say that the men who caused it aren't ever going to do anything like that again."

"I see. Are you a violent man?"

"Only when I'm pushed into it. I like to be left alone as much as possible." Even though she was putting the bandages on tightly, he didn't react to the sharp pain he felt every time she pulled the bandage around again.

"Are you married?"

He shook his head. What was she after? Why didn't she just shut up?

"Ever been married?"

He shook his head again.

"You certainly are shy or do I—"

Other Day quickly nodded. Why tell her about his life? He didn't want to get involved with her anymore than he already was. If Bull Turner hadn't kicked him in the ribs, he wouldn't be as involved as he was right then.

"Or do I detect an air of hurt about you?"

"My ribs hurt if that's what you mean," he said, wishing she would shut up and just do her job.

"I'm not talking about your ribs, Other Day. I'm talking about this."

She reached out and placed her right hand over his heart.

He wanted to yell at her to mind her own business, but he knew that if one day he were able to talk about his loss where Belle was concerned, he might be able to put it all in its right

place in his mind. But he knew he could never tell Malanie Balland about it. She looked too much like Belle Doolin. He had to find a way to get her to stop pushing for information. "Maybe one time I might tell you—but not now."

"I think I'd be willing to wait to hear your story."

"It's not a nice story."

"I didn't think it would be if you're as hurt as I think you are. How does that feel?" She stepped back and away from him, an expectant look on her face.

"Pretty good. Very good. Thank you very much."

"Let me look at your face."

"It isn't much to look at."

"I meant your wounds."

She bathed the few open cuts he had, but the swelling around the eyes had already subsided quite a bit. The discoloration was not bad, and she told him to keep the cuts that were already scabbed over clean.

She handed him his shirt. "Whenever you're ready to tell me that story, I'll be ready to listen."

Other Day looked at her and forced himself to smile. All he had to do was agree and he'd be free of having her push for it. "That sounds right promising. I'll think on it real serious."

He left the business car and went to check out the wagons and choose the one he and Theron would use to go to Ball Town. After that

he asked the driver of one of the teams to accompany them that night.

Once the preparations were finished, he went to his bedroll and lay down to rest. His ribs felt good. If he could get some sleep he'd be ready for an all night stint. He'd left instructions with the cook to tell Theron to get some rest when he came in as well. Both of them would need their wits and senses as keen as possible to enter Ball Town later that night.

CHAPTER
SIX

A late fall wind whipped across the countryside, carrying with it the hint of the first killing frost. Other Day pulled the coat he'd borrowed around him and put his head down while they rode toward Ball Town. Theron Cullen rode on the far side of the wagon and Berhardt Tigges, the mule skinner he'd chosen, sat upright and appeared impervious to the cold night air. Overhead clouds sailed high, and the dying moon soon appeared small through the thin air.

"How far is this Ball Town, Herr Logan?" Tigges asked.

"We got about another half hour to go before we leave you. All you have to do is keep the mules quiet and the wagon ready to roll once we bring the dynamite," Other Day said, puffs

of steam jetting from his mouth as he spoke.

"How far are you 'n' me goin' to have to lug that there dynamite, Other Day?" Theron asked.

"We'll take our horses to the edge of town and tie them up someplace where they won't be very noticeable. Then we'll go on foot and each bring two boxes of the stuff to the horses. We'll tie them across the backs of the saddles and bring the dynamite to the wagon. Then, we'll go back and do it all over again."

"How many trips you figure?"

"If we can get away with it and be lucky as well as quiet, I think maybe four trips. That'll give the engineer four-hundred pounds of dynamite to work with."

Theron spit. "How much those boxes weigh?"

"About twenty-five pounds a piece. Think you can carry two at a time?"

"Shoot, nothin' to it."

They fell back into silence and rode the remaining half hour. When Other Day signaled for a halt, Tigges pulled the wagon to a stop and looked around.

"Vere you vant me, Herr Logan?"

Other Day pivoted in the saddle and pointed to a grove of trees 50 yards away. "Over there. But don't go inside. Just turn the team so you can leave without having to turn them once we're ready to go. We might need the time in case someone sees us. Understand?"

"*Ja!*"

Other Day turned back to face the mule skinner. "You're German, aren't you?"

"Ja. I'm Cherman. Vhy do you ask?"

"I met a German couple a while back and I'm beholding to them. I found them to be pretty nice people." Other Day thought back to Jacob and Anna Eulberg for a moment. They had helped him when he needed it, and he never forgot people who helped him.

"Ja, Chermans are gute people." Tigges clucked to the team of mules and they responded, turning to their right and heading toward the grove of trees.

Other Day and Theron nudged their mounts in the sides and trotted away toward Ball Town. A few minutes later they reined up and dismounted. Other Day pointed to an old shed, which was the first building they encountered at the small town, and led the gelding toward it. Theron followed and they tied the two animals to an old wagon standing next to the building.

Motioning for Theron to follow him, Other Day led the way to the rear of the Gilded Garter. Keeping close to the buildings to prevent anyone from seeing their silhouettes, they hurried along, neither man making a sound as he went.

When they stood behind the saloon, they could hear a violin and banjo playing. Crowd noises filtered through the music and into the chilled night air. That was good. If there were any people about they would be busy inside,

dancing or drinking or gambling or visiting one of the painted ladies on the second floor.

Slipping around the corner, Other Day opened the shed door and entered, Theron right behind him. The 'breed left the door ajar and went to the cellar steps and hurried down after taking a stub of candle from a pile of several by the door. The door to the room where they had held him prisoner was barred, and he entered after lifting the two-by-four latch. He struck one match and held it high before lighting the candle. Turning to Theron he whispered, "Got the lay of the place?"

Theron nodded.

Other Day whispered, "I'll take from this side and you take from that." He pointed to the left side of the room and set the small candle down inside the storeroom's doorway.

Both men went to the stack of boxes they intended to work from and took two boxes. Carrying them in front of their bodies to go up the steps, they blew out the candle, closed the door, and latched it the way it had been when they first arrived. It would do no good to leave signs that someone had been there.

Outside, they shifted the boxes so they could carry them more easily and made their way to the horses. Fixing a harness of rope they hung the boxes, one on each side of the haunches, and then mounted.

Walking their horses until they were 500 yards away, they hurried them up to a canter

making certain the boxes didn't jiggle around too much.

They arrived at the wagon and unloaded. Tigges said nothing other than grunting to get into the wagon box and stack the boxes. Without a word, the two riders turned and hurried back toward Ball Town.

The second visit was as uneventful as the first, and they returned within a half hour to the wagon. The same routine was repeated, and they rode back toward the building where the dynamite was stored.

When they reached the back of the shed, they stopped and froze. They could hear voices. Theron pressed against the wall and turned to Other Day. Without speaking, both men knew what was in the mind of the other. They waited and listened intently. It was a man and a woman talking. One of the bar patrons had somehow managed to talk one of the whores into going outside, thinking he could better work a cheaper deal for himself if she weren't in the Gilded Garter.

"I can't do that, Honey. Mister Horton would be real unhappy if I did," a woman's voice said.

"Shucks, my little sweet lamb. I shore as hell ain't gonna tell him. Are you?"

"Of course not. But he'd find out just the same."

Other Day nudged Theron and shook his head. Now, because of some amorous trail-drifter or cowpoke, their own plans would be held up for a while. Other Day was a patient

man. If it took a week for the man to get the
idea through his thick skull that he wasn't
going to be successful, Other Day would wait
it out and not feel the least bit unhappy. But
they couldn't wait a week. Within a week the
rails had to be laid to Hades in order for
Balland to get the $100,000 bond money to
continue business. He'd give them a few more
minutes before exploring any alternatives to
the problem.

"Come on, Sugar," the woman said, "I gotta
get back inside, or I'll be in dutch with the
boss."

"Can't I have just one little old kiss?" the
man pleaded.

"Well—"

A short silence followed and then the man
said, "How much for upstairs?"

"I'll tell you that inside, Lover."

Other Day and Theron could hear footsteps
receding in the distance, and they both
breathed easier. Now, they could get on with
their work.

After they took their third set of four boxes,
they made their way back to their horses and
left after securing the boxes to the saddles.
When that load was deposited in the wagon,
they turned to leave.

"How many more, Herr Logan?" Tigges
asked.

"One more. Then we'll be on our way back
to the camp."

"Ja. Dot will be gute. I'm getting vorried dat someone vill come along and zee us."

"Just stay put. Anyone riding by would be lucky to see you and the rig standing there with the trees behind you."

"Ja. But hurry juzt der zame."

Other Day nodded and turned the gelding back toward Ball Town for the last trip. When they tied up, they hurried through a different route to make certain no one who might have seen them would be waiting for them. Almost a matter-of-fact routine by the fourth trip, they quickly and silently entered the shed like two shadows and made their way soundlessly down the steps to the cellar. They opened the door again and entered. After each had their two boxes, Other Day picked up the candle and they went out of the room. The 'breed set his boxes down to close the door and fix the latch in place for the last time. Just as he laid the bar in place, he stood rigid when he heard someone enter upstairs. Other Day then signaled Theron not to move.

Other Day moved to the base of the steps and listened. He could hear someone moving something around on the first floor. Why did they have to come now? A few more minutes and he and Theron would have been gone for good, their presence undetected until someone counted the boxes of dynamite. By that time it would have been too late for Horton and his gang to do anything about it.

The 'breed could hear a man grunting every time a box was slid across the floor. Then he heard a second pair of footsteps entering the room.

"What the hell's taking you so long, Calvin?"

"I'm sorry, Mr. Horton, I looked where you said, but there ain't no whiskey piled there."

"Give me your lamp," Horton said gruffly.

Other Day could hear a pair of footsteps slamming across the room.

"You looked over here?"

"I thought you meant on this side of the ro—"

"There it is you dumb ass. Now get two cases and bring it to the saloon, pronto. We've got a bunch of thirsty customers tonight."

The 'breed heard the first man grunt again when he picked up his burden and walk to the door, followed by the second man, Asa Horton. Other Day did his best to keep from going up the steps to confront and challenge the man. He had hired Bull Turner and Bull Turner had hurt Other Day's ribs. But Other Day let Horton go. He knew the day of reckoning was coming when he would have his revenge against them.

When the door closed, he moved back to the two boxes he'd set down to close the barred door and picked them up. "Let's go," he whispered to Theron, and the two men made their way up the steps for the last time. Blowing out the candle, he put it with the others.

They took their first route back to the horses and in minutes were mounted and riding back to the grove of trees.

As they approached, Other Day felt a prickly sensation on his body. Was there imminent danger close by? Why hadn't he felt anything when Horton and the other man were on the first floor of the store house? Maybe he wasn't in any real danger then. But now he was being warned by his strange alarm system that there might be danger around. He pulled back on the reins, bringing the bay gelding to a walk and slowly approached the grove. Theron followed, not asking what the matter was, but guessing that the half-breed had been alerted to something out of the ordinary.

When they turned the corner of the groove they couldn't see the wagon or the mules or Bernhardt Tigges. Where were they? What had happened?

Other Day held the bay in check and surveyed the landscape as best he could in the gloomy night. Slowly the itching sensation diminished until it was gone. What the hell was happening?

He wondered if he dare risk a call to Tigges. He listened intently and then thought he heard a scraping sound of some sort coming from within the grove itself. He prodded the horse forward and the gelding responded with a slow, quiet walk.

Other Day peered into the trees, but he could see nothing in the blackness of the shadows created by the grove.

"Tigges?" he called in a quiet voice.

"Ja?"

"Where the hell are you? Why did you

move?''

"I vought I heard zomevun coming. Zo, I moved der vagon und der mules into der grove zo nobody could zee me. Zhen, you and Herr Cullen come and I didn't know if it vaz you chentleman or not. I come out now.''

Other Day shook his head. He'd best not chastise the man for moving. If there had been someone, Tigges had done the right thing to protect the stolen dynamite and keep anyone from knowing that they were there.

When the wagon rolled out of the trees, Theron and Other Day quickly loaded their last boxes on and Tigges stacked them.

"Let's get out of here,'' the 'breed said.

"Amen, to thet, 'breed,'' Theron said. "It's gettin' a mite risky around here 'bouts.''

"Ja. Ve go. I'm getting skittish around here,'' Tigges said and slapped the reins over the rumps of the team.

They rode in silence, each man lost in his own thoughts. The animals jetted clouds of steam into the cold night air, and the only sound other than the slow beat of the hooves on the cold ground was the creaking of the wagon. The noises slipped out into the night and were soon lost in the quie

Other Day took a deep breath and thanked Melanie Balland in a silent salute for the good job she'd done wrapping his ribs. He pulled the borrowed coat tighter around him and concentrated on guiding his small entourage back to

the end-of-track camp. Tomorrow, they had to blow half of a hill into a ravine to level off the ground so the laying of track could continue into Hades.

CHAPTER
SEVEN

Other Day rolled and tossed in his sleeping bag as two Belle Doolins confronted him in his dreams. Or were there two Melanie Ballands? Both gazed at him adoringly and held out their arms to him. He shook his head and opened his mouth to speak. A loud explosion erupted and he sat up, wide awake. What the hell had that noise been?

He looked around and found Theron sitting up in his bedroll, rubbing his eyes and yawning.

"What the hell was that?" Other Day asked.

"I don't know. I just woke up when I heard it."

"I wonder—of course," Other Day said, "they're blasting the hill with the dynamite we brought into camp this morning."

The 'breed stretched and got to his feet. Pulling the canvas cover over his bedroll, he suddenly realized how cold it was. The ground was still covered with frost, even though the sun shined through some of the heavy clouds. He shook his head. This was not his idea of comfortable weather, and it would only get worse. As soon as the first train pulled into Hades, he would head back south. He might go to Texas or to the New Mexico Territory. Sure it could snow there but the air was different— not nearly so cold as it was where he was right then. He stooped and picked up the loaned coat and put it on.

"Come on, Theron. Enough rest. Let's ride to where they're blasting. I want to see if it's working. If it is, there should be no problem getting to Hades on time."

Theron pulled out a plug of tobacco and bit off a hunk. "Sure," he said chomping down on the chew, "but I gotta get goin' or the cook'll have my hide. He's only got enough meat fer today." He rolled to one side, covered his bedroll and stood. When he stood up, Theron ran to catch up to Other Day, who was heading toward the cook car.

Once they had drunk a cup of hot coffee, they went to the tether line and saddled their horses. Swinging onto the backs of their mounts, they rode toward the west. Clouds of steam puffed out of the animals' nostrils as they cantered.

When Other Day and Theron rode up, they found Henry Balland, his daughter Melanie,

and Dismus Scott standing together examining the results of the blast that had awakened the 'breed and the hunter.

The dynamite crew was setting more charges on the freshly wounded hillside, and Other Day rode past the last knot of people at the lip of the ravine and looked down. Earth, rocks, and debris covered the remains of the trestle that had lain at the bottom, not unlike some broken skeleton. He turned the bay and walked him back to the superintendent.

"Will it work?" he asked.

Before Henry Balland could answer, Dismus Scott spoke up. "Aye. It'll work and then some. I think two more charges should fill the ravine and then we can set the grading crew to work smoothing it out."

"Other Day," Balland said, "you'll never know how much I'm in your debt. Without that idea, we'd be packing up and heading back toward Ashton right now."

"Aye," Scott said. "It was a brilliant innovation. I'm only sorry I didn't think of it myself."

Other Day swung down from the gelding and walked over to them. He felt almost embarrassed. He didn't like people to feel they were obligated to him in any way. He had had an idea, and it happened to have worked out for the good of the project. It could just as easily have not worked.

Before he could say anything, Melanie walked up to him. "Father and I will be forever grateful, Other Day. How are your ribs

feeling?"

Other Day felt a rush of blood rising to his face. Maybe he should just tell them to stop it right now. He wanted no more accolades nor comments of concern thrown his way. "My ribs are feeling fine."

"Didn't they hurt this morning when you woke up—considering the cold temperature?" she asked, standing in his way to prevent him from walking closer to her father.

"No. They feel fine. They really do," he said, sidestepping the woman.

Theron Cullen walked his pinto and mule over to the group and said, "Well, since it's workin', I'll vamoose and get a huntin'. The way the cook was talkin' this mornin', I'll be shot at sunset if I don't get some meat for his pot. See you later, Other Day."

"Right," the 'breed said, touching the brim of his Stetson.

Theron turned his mount and rode away, the pack mule in tow.

Turning his attention back to Balland, the 'breed said, "How do you stand now with the miles left to go and so on."

"It should be no problem now that we've solved the matter of replacing the trestle. The end of track is three miles behind us and the grading crew is only one mile away. We've got sixteen miles to go in the next four days. We should make it to Hades with no more problems. Of course, the cold weather and

ground freezing isn't going to make it any easier."

Other Day felt a surge of discomfort pass over his body. His warning sign. Without being obvious, he turned in a full circle over the next couple of minutes to survey the landscape. He saw nothing and wondered if what Balland had said might have triggered the reaction. Did that mean they would still have problems before they reached the town of Hades? Or was there an immediate threat of some sort?

When he finished his perusal of the countryside, he turned back to the others and found Melanie smiling at him.

"Is there something funny?" he asked.

"No. I was just wondering why you wear a headband. I wanted to ask you when I was bandaging your ribs but didn't."

"My mother gave it to me."

"Your mother?"

"She was a Pawnee princess. She made it for me when she wasn't allowed to return to her people after my father died. Pawnees don't wear headbands like mine and she felt that I should wear one and be my own man, not part of the white community nor of the Pawnee."

Melanie blushed. "I'm sorry. I didn't know there was that sort of reason."

"Melanie," her father said, "let me and Mr. Logan and Mr. Scott here talk. You promised you wouldn't be a bother."

"Oh, Father," she said and turned to walk

away.

"Don't go far, Miss Balland," Scott said. "They'll be blowing more of the hill in a few minutes. I see the men are coming this way now."

Scott herded the Ballands and Other Day toward a small hillock nearby and they sought protection there from any far-flying debris that might strike them. Other Day led the gelding toward the same protection where the other mounts were tied.

"We're ready," someone yelled from a short distance away. "Everyone stay down."

A thick silence fell over the people huddling behind the small hills, and then the booming explosion shook the earth.

Other Day raised his head enough to see what was happening. A pointed finger of black dirt, rock, and dust moved skyward for a moment before falling to the earth in the direction of the partially filled ravine. The sound of rocks and dirt falling to the earth sounded like a heavy rain storm pelting the ground. When that sound died down, everyone stood.

Moving toward the edge of the gulley, they found the earth almost up to the top.

"Aye," Scott yelped. "It's beautiful. One more and we can begin leveling it off."

"Mr. Scott?" Balland said.

"Aye?"

"Will the earth be settled enough for us to lay track and take a train across?"

"Aye, that's a good question. We may have

to put more than the usual amount of ballast beneath the track. Everyone should think of a way to maybe build a support that would take any fear of trouble away."

"A support?" Balland asked.

"Aye. Perhaps we could sink rail perpendicular to the track every so often to support different ties. That would probably do it."

"That sounds reasonable, Mr. Scott. Plan on doing it if it proves necessary." Balland turned to Other Day. "As for you, Mr. Logan, you can plan on some sort of bonus for your ingenuity."

"That's not necessary, Mr. Balland." He turned and walked toward the bay and mounted.

"Can you go to the grading crew and have them start up here with the teams and earth scoop to finish this job, Other Day?" Balland called.

"Sure," Other Day said and spurred the gelding toward the grading site.

Later that afternoon, while riding in the general direction of the town of Hades, Other Day pulled up beneath a large cottonwood tree and rested his horse for a moment. He'd been riding a zigzag trail, crisscrossing the intended route of the L.A.& H.'s mainline. He wanted to know if there might be any place that could cause trouble or be a possible ambush site in the event Horton and his men decided to try to stop them in a way more permanent than the

methods they'd used up to that time. He wondered if they'd discovered the missing dynamite yet.

Based on Balland and Scott's assessment of the situation, there wasn't much Horton could do now that the gulley was being filled. That was the last natural obstacle that Horton could use as a weapon against the Balland people.

The bay nickered and Other Day sat up alert. The horse looked off toward the southern horizon, and Other Day did the same after he stood up. He saw two riders heading south and east toward Ball Town, which was the only inhabited place in that direction for miles. He wondered who they might be. From the way they rode, they had apparently not seen him. If they were Horton's men, he'd just as soon not have a confrontation out there in the wilds. If his ribs were in good shape, he'd have no objection to meeting some of those men anywhere. But right then he wanted to let his cracked ribs heal. In time, he'd meet up with Bull Turner and pay him in kind for the pain and suffering he'd given the 'breed.

If the two riders, who were out of sight now, were Horton's men, where had they been and what had they been up to in that part of the country? Logan's body hadn't itched when he was first aware of them or even before; so he felt he was in no immediate danger himself. Still, his curiosity ran rampant, and he felt that maybe he should follow them just to see who they were and where they were going. But he

felt his first duty was to Balland who had sent him out to check for possible ambush sites. He'd found none that would prove to be an imminent threat, but there were more rocky bluffs and hillsides to the north a few miles away. That was almost out of the range of a Winchester, and it would take a superb marksman with some sort of scope to hit anything at that distance. A man or horse wasn't all that big from that distance.

He had ridden to the bluffs and found several natural caves, but dismissed them when he calculated how far away the proposed mainline was from there.

He walked over to the bay and mounted, patting him on the neck. The gelding was a good horse and he would be eternally grateful to G. Ridley Thorne for having furnished him with such a fine animal. So what if Thorne were going to jail for a long time because of his dealings with outlaws while working for the government. He had still been responsible for paying for the horse, and that was all that concerned Other Day. Turning the animal's head east, he clucked to him and the horse stepped out.

It was almost supper time when he reached the camp, and the men were milling around outside the kitchen car. Obediah Johnson stood in the door, his white apron acting like a beacon in the encroaching darkness.

"There ain't no damned meat here," he screamed.

Other Day rode over when he heard the man yell that. Where was Theron? Why hadn't he come back to camp with meat for the day?

"Hey, cook?" he yelled over the clamor of the hungry working men.

"What?"

"Hasn't Theron come back yet?"

"No, he hasn't, but if he does, I'm gonna give him a pants fulla buckshot, by Gawd. He shoulda been back here hours ago. These men are hungry and all I can give 'em is pancakes."

"Pancakes?" the men yelled. "We want meat. Not breakfast food."

"Hold on, men," Other Day yelled out. "You all know Theron. You know he's pretty darn reliable. If he hasn't come in yet with meat, it's because he ran into some sort of problem. Eat whatever the cook here can give you and I'll try to back track Theron."

"In the dark?" someone yelled and several men laughed derisively.

Other Day turned and stared down at the man who had spoken. The man blanched under the withering glare of the half-breed and an uncomfortable silence fell over the group. When the man realized he'd insulted the troubleshooter, he turned away, a shamed look on his face.

Other Day looked at the cook. "I'll try to find him and bring him and the meat back."

He reined the gelding to the left and rode out of the darkening camp. All he knew was Theron had headed northeast when he had left the

blasting site earlier that day. That would mean that if he continued in a straight line toward the hilly country north of end-of-track camp he might be there or someplace in between. Instead of riding to the old trestle site, Logan elected to ride due north. Some instinct, some urge made him turn that way, and he rode off as fast as he would allow the bay to go at night.

If Theron were in trouble he wanted to be the one to help him. He liked Theron. There was a special quality about the man, and Other Day knew that Theron Cullen would do the same for him if their positions were reversed.

By the time he reached the first of the hilly country to the north, night had already fallen and the quarter moon rose high in the cold, clear night. Other Day breathed a sigh of thanks that at least he could have some degree of help from the moonlight.

He froze when his body began itching again and he heard slow hoof beats of an animal walking toward him. The day had been humid, and there was frost already forming on the grass and low growing brushes and scrub trees.

Holding the bay in check, he waited. The gelding nickered quietly and Other Day tried to quiet him. Instead, he heard a mule bray back in answer.

"Theron?" he called out and rode toward the sound of the mule. In seconds he found the animal with two large buck deer tied across its back. He grabbed the rope and yelled out again, "Theron?"

No answer. His body continued itching, the sensation building with each passing moment. He leaped off the horse and took the lead rope of the pack mule and tied it to a scrub tree.

Studying the ground, he found the mule's tracks were quite clearly marked in the frost whitened grass.

Remounting, he started backtracking the mule. While he kept his eyes on the ground, he rubbed at his chest with his left hand. Something was wrong someplace. Danger or something lay ahead. He had to find Theron.

CHAPTER
EIGHT

Other Day rode through the blue-white country, head bent down studying the dark trail in the frosty grass. The mule had wandered about for quite some time from what he could tell. Because he followed the erratic trail of the pack animal first east, then south, then northwest and then north again, he was losing time. The trail was slowly whitening to match its surroundings. If he lost the trail, despite the relatively bright light of the quarter moon, he might search the rest of the night and never find Theron.

As he rode, he absently rubbed his chest, trying to relieve the tingling that had manifested when he found Theron's pack mule with the two buck deer. The warning signal had con-

tinued, growing in its intensity. It mounted in degrees as he rode, and he was aware that the trail was slowly disappearing because of the ever-falling temperature.

He spurred the bay forward at a faster pace. Normally he wouldn't push any mount that fast at night, but the moon was bright and reflected off the whitened grass and shrubs, adding to the illumination.

When the bay cocked his ears forward, Other Day pulled up. The horse had heard something. Straining his own hearing, he listened intently. He could hear nothing at the moment. That didn't mean that the gelding hadn't heard something. In order to use his sense of hearing even more, he decided to ride slower and keep the noise the horse made at a minimum while he made his way through the crisp grass and bushes.

Then he and the horse heard the noise at the same time. The gelding nickered and Other Day pulled up. He'd heard a horse whinny. In answer to the bay's nicker, another whinny sounded and Other Day stood up in the stirrups.

"Theron? Theron Cullen? Is that you? Answer me!"

A whispering breeze wound through the pine trees to his left, but he heard no answer. Clucking to the gelding, they moved forward slowly. He didn't want to run the risk of riding right past his friend, in the event Theron couldn't answer for some reason.

The gelding nickered again and then whinnied loudly. An answering whinny much louder than before sounded from the 'breed's right. He turned in that direction and headed toward a grove of trees. the largest one he'd passed since finding the mule.

Facing it as he rode, he called out again, "Theron? Is that you? Answer me, Theron."

The horse's hoof sounds were muffled in the tall grass, and Other Day could hear nothing else. If Theron were in the grove, he either wasn't answering, or was unable to.

Logan rode to the edge of the trees and peered in. He could see nothing. Dismounting, he led the horse in, past a large birch tree. The moonlight reflected off the white bark and frosty grass around the perimeter of the grove. But inside, where the ground was protected from the dew and cold by the canopy of leaves of the birch and cottonwood trees, no frost had formed yet and it became more dark than out in the open.

The gelding inadvertently stepped on a fallen branch and the resounding snap sounded like a rifle shot. The horse they'd heard whickered again. The animal was close.

Other Day wanted to call Theron's name again, but decided not to since he wasn't sure if it was Theron Cullen's pinto responding to the gelding. He might be running the risk of stalking the camp of another hunter who might not take kindly to a stranger sneaking up on him in the middle of the night. It might also be

some of Asa Horton's men camped out keeping an eye on the L.A. & H.'s activity.

Dropping the reins, he ground tied the gelding and went ahead on foot. He moved like a specter through the darkened grove of trees. No sound came from his feet as he moved. Only an occasional dribble of frosty steam escaped his nose while he controlled his breathing for fear of making too much noise. As though his feet had eyes, he avoided without looking down fallen branches and twigs. Leaves that should have made a rustling sound as he passed lay perfectly still despite the boots walking through them.

When he came to a large birch tree blocking his way, he stopped and looked in all directions to make certain he hadn't missed anything.

Then, he saw the pinto tied to a small birch. The horse realized he'd been found and that the 'breed's eyes had fallen on him. He whickered a greeting.

Walking in that direction, Other Day still passed over the floor of the grove without making a sound. When he stood ten feet from the horse, he saw the body hanging from one of the trees behind the pinto.

"Theron?" he cried out and ran to his friend.

Theron hung by his wrists from a branch overhead. His buckskin coat, wool shirt and long underwear top had been torn off. His head hung down to one side. Other Day turned the hanging body to look at the face. When he did,

he confirmed that it was Theron hanging there. Deep bloody lash marks crisscrossed his back and chest. His face was a mask of dried blood. When Other Day saw a whisp of steam jet from his nostrils and mouth, he quickly lifted Theron's body with his left arm and reached behind his neck, pulling out the razor-sharp throwing knife. The blade sliced through the rope holding Theron, and his full weight crashed onto Other Day's left arm. Catching the off-balanced load in both arms, careful not to cut his friend anymore than he already had been, he gently lowered Theron to the ground.

Theron moaned and Other Day stood up. "Stay there, my friend. I'll get a blanket and make you warm before I light a fire."

The hunter made no response, and Other Day turned and ran lightly through the trees to where he'd left the gelding. Bringing him to the small clearing where he'd found Theron, he ground tied him again and took the small blanket he had in the saddle bags and wrapped Theron's upper body in it. Then he quickly gathered small branches and built a fire. Within minutes, he had a warm blaze lighting the clearing, and he looked at Theron's wounds after moving him closer to the warmth. He brought his canteen from the saddle and placed it near Theron.

The hunter shivered and Other Day recovered the deep lacerations with the blanket. He couldn't tend to them there

without proper bandages and sufficient water. He had no idea where there might be water around, and he felt he couldn't take the time to look for any. All he could do was make Theron comfortable until he either got strong enough to ride or— Other Day shook his head. He didn't even want to think about the alternatives.

What was wrong with him? Did he carry a mark from the gods of the Pawnee? A curse that deemed anyone who befriended Other Day Logan would die a horrible death. He thought back to his mother. She had been his only friend outside of Father McGhee when he'd been growing up. Then Half-Ear Hantelmann had brutally murdered her after raping her. Other Day had other friends over the years, although not too many since he preferred his solitude. But each of them had also met untimely ends. The worst situation was Belle Doolin, whom he thought he'd loved and who had been raped and murdered by Ike Furlong. Both Hantelmann and Furlong had paid with their lives at the hands of Other Day.

Now it was going to happen again. He needn't try to fool himself. He knew that Theron was as good as dead. He would have a hard time recovering from the multiple wounds that had been inflicted on him even if there were adequate bandages and medicine to help him. But Other Day knew nothing of tending wounds such as Theron's, and he certainly had no

medicine or bandages with which to help his friend.

Other Day stood. Maybe he carried a bad luck omen on him. No. That was the white man's answer for bad luck and that was stupid. His first thought, the mark from the gods, was Pawnee crap. He tended not to believe in either side's superstitions or creeds. He had his own.

Then he stopped and thought for a moment. Father McGhee. Father David McGhee was his friend and nothing had ever happened to him. He thought of the round-shouldered, bespectacled priest. His forthright manner had won him many friends over the years. His hearty laugh and pudgy build stood out as being totally unsuited for life on the Oklahoma frontier. And still the man had survived, dealing with white settlers and Indians alike. He'd befriended Careche-Coranche, Other Day's Pawnee princess mother, when she and her husband Joshua Logan first came to the Oklahoma territory from the Nebraska frontier. The priest had given Other Day, whom he had baptized with the mistaken name, his education and moral support and guidance when Careche-Coranche had been murdered.

Other Day smiled. Every once in a while he found himself drawing on some of the priest's wisdom.

He looked down at Theron. The man's face twisted in pain and the puffs of steam came

in erratic clouds as he fought to stay alive. Then suddenly his eyes opened, darting about and stopping when he saw Other Day.

Squirming, he tried to sit up and whispered, "No more. No more whip. Let me alone. I ain't done nuthin."

"Easy, my friend," the 'breed said softly and gently pushed Theron back onto the ground. "Theron? Can you hear me?"

"Huh? Who is it?"

"Other Day. Other Day Logan. The half-breed. Do you know me?"

"Sure. Where the hell you been? I coulda used you a few hours ago." Theron's voice sounded a bit stronger and his eyes became more alert.

"What happened? Who did this to you?" Other Day looked up for an instant, and his eyes focused on something he'd completely overlooked in his haste to care for the hunter. Theron's bull-whip lay, stretched out like a black snake in the grass and weeds on the far side of Theron. How had he overlooked it? Someone had used his own whip on him. But why?

"Big man. Lots bigger 'n you, Other Day. Him and another guy come ridin' by about the middle of the afternoon. At first, they seemed right friendly-like but then the big one all of a sudden pulls his gun and says to his partner, 'Tie him up and string 'im from a tree.' They dragged me in here and tied me so's my feet

just cleared the ground, and the feller who tied me up pulls off half my clothes, and the big guys says, 'What's the railroad people doin' blastin' the way they are?' I told him. I told him good too how you and me stole their dynamite and how Horton's gonna lose now that the gorge is filled up."

Other Day grabbed the canteen and lifted Theron's head to give him a drink. The injured man choked on the water at first, but he took a bit more when he stopped coughing.

"Take it easy, Theron. We got nothing but time."

"Maybe you have, 'breed, but not me. I think this is it."

"You're not that bad off," Other Day said, forcing himself to lie. "Your wounds aren't that bad."

"Don't try to shit an old turd like me, Other Day. I know how I feel and I ain't never felt like this 'fore in my life. No, sir. It's all over." His voice grew weaker.

"Did these men use names? Was one called Bull?"

Theron nodded and a pained look crossed his face. "That's the man. He done the whippin'. Used my friend to do it, too. Thet don't hardly seem right somehow."

"Don't fret none about that, Theron. I'll settle any differences you might have with them."

"You be careful, son. He's a mean one."

"I know. We've had a couple of run-ins

already and right now the score is tied. The next time'll be for everything."

"Whatcha mean?" Theron slurred, his voice growing weaker.

"Don't worry about it. Get some sleep. I'll take you back to the camp in the morning."

"You won't be tak—" His voice died away and his head fell a bit to the right. Theron was dead.

Other Day didn't move. A snarling growl, sounding like distant thunder, rumbled deep within his chest. He stared at the dead man for a long time and then stood to go around the body and over to the whip on the ground. He picked up the handle and pulled the fifteen-foot length from the grass. Slowly coiling it, he slung it over his left shoulder when he finished. He had an appointment with Bull Turner that would be coming up soon. He'd go directly into Ball Town and challenge him to come out into the street if need be. No matter where or when, sometime soon Other Day Logan would meet up with him and Theron Cullen's death would be avenged.

The 'breed looked down at Theron. He'd been a bit less than smart in telling Bull about their stealing the dynamite. Bull was probably sore about Other Day's escape from the dynamite room in the first place. He knew the big man harbored nothing but hate for him because of their first encounter when Other Day had totally embarrassed him in front of the grading crew.

"Sleep well, friend. You're going to have nothing but a full larder from your hunting now when you get where it is you're going. Sleep well."

Other Day brought the pinto closer to Theron's body and ground tied him. Picking up Theron by the arm pits, he hoisted him to a standing position and then lifted him, sliding the body over the saddle. When he was sure the dead man was riding comfortably, he tied his hands and feet together to make certain he wouldn't jostle and fall from the saddle.

After stamping out the fire, he picked up the reins of the pinto and walked over to the gelding. He swung into the saddle and turned the bay to leave the grove. He knew approximately where he'd left the mule and its cargo of deer. He only hoped that there weren't any cats or bear in the area. If there were, and they found the mule, there might be a hunger revolt in the camp because of the lack of meat for the workers.

Thirty minutes later, he found the mule and the meat intact. He retrieved the lead rope and remounted, guiding the pinto and its dead cargo and the mule and its life-giving cargo toward the south and the end-of-track camp.

An hour and a half later, he walked the bay, the pinto, and the mule into camp. A quiet calm hung over the work train. For an instant, he looked up on the hillside to the south where he and Theron had slept outside at night. He could

see the two bedrolls standing out in stark relief against the white frost.

Other Day shook his head and rode toward the kitchen car. He awakened the cook and turned the mule and the two field-dressed bucks over to him. He looked at Theron's body and sleepily shook his head yawning and climbed down to take charge of the meat.

Continuing along the length of the work train, the 'breed came to the business car at the end. After a moment's hesitation he decided it would be best to tell Henry Balland about Theron at that time rather than wait until morning. He dismounted and climbed aboard at the rear platform. He knocked quietly and waited.

Nothing happened and he knocked again. This time his keen hearing picked up the sound of someone coming. A coal oil lamp's soft light bobbed along the passageway, and in a moment, Henry Balland entered the office at the rear of the business car.

Holding the lamp high, he saw who stood at the door through the window and quickly turned the knob. "Come in, Other Day. What did you find?"

Other Day motioned for him to come out onto the platform.

Large puffs of steam squirted from Henry Balland's nosrils when he saw the body of Theron Cullen draped across his pinto. He motioned with his head for Other Day to enter

the car, then he closed the door once the 'breed was inside.

"What in God's name happened? How'd his back get that way?"

Other Day told him how he found Theron and how the hunter was able to tell him what had happened before he died. When he finished, he waited for a moment and then told Balland. "I think I might have seen Bull and the other man yesterday afternoon. I was west of here and saw them from a distance. I couldn't make out who they were, but now that I've thought on it, the one man had to be Bull Turner. He's pretty big and stands out even at a distance of a mile."

"You didn't follow them?" Balland asked.

"No, sir. They were riding like hell toward the southeast. I suppose to Ball Town since there isn't anything else down that way for quite a piece."

"I wonder why they went in that roundabout way?" Balland pulled his robe around his body even tighter.

"Probably they were spying on the blasting yesterday morning and then happened to run into Theron. When they found out what was going on and where we got the dynamite, they decided to check out his story. If the gulley's filled up, you have nothing to prevent you from reaching Hades on time and receiving the bond money. They're probably making plans right now to keep you from doing just that, Mister Balland."

Balland nodded. "You're probably right. You'd best get some sleep. Have two of the men who are standing guard bury Theron. I'll need you as soon as you can get up in the morning to organize a squad of outriders who can keep U.L. & B.T. men at bay while we continue to lay track. Confound it, why couldn't Asa Horton have stayed out of it?"

Other Day shrugged.

"I'm sending someone for the territorial marshal first thing in the morning," Balland said. "With you as a witness to Theron's statement, we can at least have this Bull Turner arrested. With him out of the picture Horton's crew might be disorganized long enough for us to reach Hades."

"Considering all the problems you're having reaching Hades, I imagine I might get a good seat in heaven after all the things I've done," Other Day said and turned to leave. He heard Balland laugh a bit, and then he was outside in the bitter cold once more. He wasn't going to sleep. He had something important to do. There were at least three hours before sunrise and he couldn't sleep under the circumstances. The hatred he felt building in him for Bull Turner piled on top of the dislike he had for what Bull had done to him. Now, Bull had killed Theron Cullen, and Other Day was going to have to balance the scales of justice once more. He wanted to get a hold of Bull Turner before the marshal did. If that happened and Bull wound up in jail, Other Day would never

get at him. He couldn't allow that to happen.

After he told two of the night guards to dig a grave for Theron, he woke two men and appointed them hunters to take Theron's place. It would take two to replace him.

Then Other Day mounted the gelding and rode out of the camp with Theron Cullen's bullwhip draped over his left shoulder. He had to practice.

CHAPTER
NINE

Other Day turned away from the cottonwood tree and stepped off a dozen paces. Facing the tree, he picked out the twig with the birch leaf tied to it. The golden leaf stood out from those of the cottonwood that hadn't yet fallen. Slipping the whip from his shoulder, he threw it out behind him and then sighted on the foreign leaf in front of him again. Picturing Bull Turner in his mind, he imagined that the leaf was Bull's nose. His right hand went into motion and the tip of the long, snake-like whip moved. At the precise moment that it would have cut through the leaf, he arrested the popper's flight, and the resounding crack snapped the leaf to bits with its concussion. He brought the whip back again, lightning fast,

its tip shot out again, snapping off another, this time a cottonwood leaf. Again the whip snaked behind Other Day and shot out, taking a branch on which the 'breed had set his sight.

When he stopped, a slow, almost evil smile crossed his mouth. He was ready. He'd spent the better part of six hours working with the whip. He felt he was good enough to hold his own with the whip if he had to—almost as good as Theron had been. He wasn't sure if he could take on a grizzly the way Theron had, but if he had to, he would.

The half-breed looped the whip and placed it over his left shoulder. The only thing he didn't like about the whip was that it took a second or two to unwind it. He didn't think he'd ever get into a situation where he would have to be the faster of two in unwinding and getting his bullwhip ready to defend himself. If it took him time, it would take another man time to prepare as well.

He found the bay grazing and removed the horse's hobble. It would take a couple of hours to ride back to the end-of-track camp. He had purposely gone far enough to be out of earshot of the camp. He didn't want the men in camp wondering what the cracking was. He knew it sounded not unlike a rifle shot at a distance if the whip were worked properly.

"I sure been working you hard, boy," he said to the horse, patting him on the neck.

The gelding whickered at the sound of Other Day's voice.

The 'breed had not taken the saddle off. Although he knew he should have, he had planned on practicing with the whip for several hours and wanted to be prepared to ride at an instant's notice if any of Horton's men—Bull Turner especially—showed up unexpectedly.

After mounting, he looked at the sun, which was much lower in the sky than it had been a week or so before, and estimated that it was mid-morning. Winter was coming, and he wanted to get out of that part of the country. He didn't care much for snow. He preferred sunshine and warmth to overcast skies and cold. As long as he was alone, he could do what he wanted, when he wanted, and he did not have to worry about what someone else might want. He clucked to the bay and moved out toward camp.

Other Day recalled when he was growing up, before the death of his mother, how the Cherokee Indian children tried to make friendly overtures to him. He knew they were of another tribe but he also knew that he wasn't a full-blooded Indian, or, for that matter, a full-blooded white. He had found he preferred his own company as a child, a youth, and as a man. Somehow he had gotten tied up with the railroad and Henry Balland and his daughter Melanie. He wasn't so very involved with them, but he wouldn't be able to ride away without

regrets. If he would have one, it would be that he wouldn't be able to see Melanie and think of Belle Doolin. While the resemblance was remarkable, they were nothing alike.

He continued thinking of Melanie and Belle while he rode. When he was a mile from camp, he pulled up. He thought he heard something. Listening carefully, he nodded almost perceptibly. A rifle shot. He *had* heard something.

Spurring the bay with his heels, he rode ahead toward the camp. When he approached the last hill before he would be able to see the camp, he reined up and turned to the left. There was a draw there in which he could ride closer without being seen along the horizon. Picking his way through the rocky floor of the draw, Other Day slowed even more when he was almost in the open.

He peered out carefully and saw no activity. There had been other shots while he rode nearer, but now there was nothing but silence. He could see no movement around the work train, and there was no one working on the track crew. Just as he rode clear of the protective hill, another shot rang out. He ducked in the saddle but got the bay galloping ahead full tilt in a matter of two or three seconds. The horse slid to a stop on his hind legs, rearing up partway as Other Day swung down from the saddle. The 'breed threw himself on the ground and rolled over to where Hold Riggs, the grading crew foreman, lay

hidden behind a truck of one of the storage cars.

"What's going on?" Other Day asked when he was equally protected.

"There's a couple of men north of here taking potshots at us. Not real often, mind you, but whenever someone moves they take a random shot. We've been pinned down here since dawn," Riggs said.

"No one's done any work yet?"

"No sir."

"Where's Balland?"

"Down by the kitchen car, I think."

Other Day wanted to ask where Melanie was but decided she must be out of danger in the business car where she and her father had sleeping quarters.

The 'breed scrambled to his feet and, crouching, dashed along the south side of the work train toward the kitchen car. A shot rang out but the slug kicked up dirt 20 feet behind him. It was apparent that they weren't really trying to hit him, but rather to scare him into not moving around too much. But Other Day didn't want to play that game. He was going to introduce a couple of new rules. First, he wanted to talk with Balland.

He found the superintendent crouched behind a row of barrels. When the 'breed dashed up and ducked behind a hogshead, Balland looked up startled and said, "I thought I gave orders for everyone to stay put until the

firing was over. Why didn't— Other Day. Where have you been, man? We've got troubles here."

"I see that. Why did you tell everyone to lay low? You'll never get your railroad built that way. How are you doing mile-wise and time-wise?"

Balland relaxed a little when he realized it was the 'breed who had ducked behind the barrels. "At the end of work yesterday, we had sixteen miles to go. Counting today, we have four days to do it. And," he added, "we've already lost a fourth of a day just lying here waiting for someone to say it's all right for us to go back to work."

"If those are Horton's men—and I'm sure they are—I don't think you'll be receiving permission soon. I'll try to circle around and come up from behind them. Maybe I can catch them off guard."

"I'm not sure if I should let you do that," Balland said angrily. "They've already wounded two men. Nothing serious, but damn it, I'm ready to explode myself."

"Do you think you could stop me?"

Balland jerked up and stared at the half-breed. "I—I didn't mean anything by that, Other Day, I—"

"I know you didn't, Mr. Balland. You're a nice man and a good railroad man. The likes of Horton and his bunch aren't your kind at all. They're mine. You take care of the railroad and I'll take care of them. Fair enough deal?"

Balland's eyes softened and he smiled. "You're quite a judge of character, aren't you? Ever since this trouble started, I haven't been able to begin to understand why they're doing this."

"For the money and to prove they're tougher and bigger than you and your outfit. That's all."

"You make it sound so simple."

"It is simple and they're simple and I'll take care of them. Does anyone here have an idea as to how many there might be out there?"

"The first shot came close to one of the mule skinners, Tigges. He yelled over to me before that there were only two of them out there."

"Where's he at?"

"Over there," Balland said, pointing toward a stack of railroad ties that were more exposed than most of the camp.

Other Day studied the position and decided he'd best use his horse to get there. Getting to his feet, he ran, bent over, along the length of the work train again, back to where he'd left his horse by Riggs. In order to use the gelding as a shield, he'd have to hang on the right-hand side of the saddle. He wondered if the horse would permit that. Working his way around, he approached the animal and talked to him. The gelding whickered quietly in response.

Other Day put his left foot in the right stirrup and pulled himself up, grabbing the withers. The horse didn't move.

"Giddyup," Other Day said softly.

The horse moved out and from the north it

appeared as though a saddled horse was walking around unattended. When Logan reached the ties where Tigges was pinned down, he stopped the horse, but stayed hanging on the side.

"How many guns are firing?" the 'breed asked.

"*Ja!* Dere are two men chooting at us. Dey take turns."

"Are they close together—at the same spot?"

"*Nein.* Vun is behind a big rock outcropping und der udder is behind zum trees to der vest of der rocks."

"I think I know where you mean. Stay put for a while longer."

"*Ja!* You couldn't get me out here mit a team of mules," Tigges said.

Other Day clucked to the gelding and he moved out to the east. No shots were taken at the horse, and the half-breed waited until the bay entered a depressed area between two hillocks before dropping off the right side and swinging into the saddle from the left.

He headed east for several miles before heading north and west, making sure that he would come up from behind the men who had concealed themselves about a quarter of a mile north of the train. The terrain was such that he had to ride that far out of his way in order not to be seen by the Horton men.

The hard, frozen ground sounded the bay's hoofs striking, and Logan hoped he'd be able to get close enough to the men without having

to walk too fast. The farther he had to walk, the more likelihood of them seeing him.

He pulled up the gelding and dismounted. A rifle shot rang out again, and he pinpointed it about 200 yards to the south of his location. Leading the bay, he walked toward the sound.

A few minutes later, he heard another shot and knew it was time to tie the gelding. Proceeding on foot, he ducked from tree to rock to outcropping to tree, moving without making a sound despite the thick rug of fallen leaves, which he encountered every once in a while near groves of trees.

When the next shot rang out, he saw the man and calculated that only 30 or 40 yards separated him from the man. He inches his way forward, slipping the whip from his left shoulder and moving it to his right hand.

Snake-like, Other Day slithered through the brush separating him from the nearest man. All he wanted was one of them. If one got away, it would make no difference. In fact, it might serve his interests well if one did get away, taking back the story that his partner had been taken prisoner. Maybe it would deter the Horton camp from doing anything for a while and more progress on the L.A. & H.'s mainline could be made.

When he was within 15 feet of the man, he studied the situation. He was to the rifleman's left. He looked overhead. No low hanging branches. Uncoiling the whip, he let it drop to the ground. He had to get the tip and length

airborne before making a hit at the man.

Bringing his right hand and arm up, he got the whip in motion. Slicing through the air, it sounded like a wind blowing. The man looked up and around, but before he could react, the tip of the bullwhip lashed out and smacked him in the face.

The man dropped his rifle and it discharged into the ground. He screamed out in pain, and Other Day hurled himself at the wounded man. They both fell to the ground when the impact of the 'breed's body struck the other man, and before he could regain his balance or composure, the half-breed had knocked him out with the butt of his Colt .44.

"Hey? Highpockets? You all right?" the other gunman called out.

Other Day made no sound.

"Highpockets? What was that noise?"

Other Day waited to see if the man would investigate or spook and run. In seconds, he heard crashing footsteps through the brush and leaves as the other man dashed for his own safety.

The 'breed smiled. Whites got so damned scared when it came to not being able to understand something. If Logan knew anything, the running man was probably doing something in his drawers while he ran for his life.

Taking out a length of rope, he tied the injured man's hands and dragged him toward a tree. Once Other Day had him strung up from a branch, his feet just touching the ground, he

slapped the man in the face, bringing him around.

"What were you shooting at the work crew for?"

The man narrowed his eyes and smiled. "You're pretty dumb, half-breed, if you can't figure that out. Horton and Turner and their gang will stop that damned road somehow. They got plans."

Other Day stepped closer. "You mean you work for Horton and he told you to shoot at those people down there?"

"Yup."

"Tell me about their plans."

"I dunno. I just do what I'm told."

"I know you, don't I?"

"How should I know?"

Other Day glared at him. "You're the man who told Bull Turner that I was in the Gilded Garter a couple of days ago."

"So what if I did, what are you gonna do about it?"

The 'breed chuckled. "And you think I'm dumb? You're the one tied up hanging from a tree, and I'm the one with the bullwhip. Because of your big mouth, Bull managed to break a couple of my ribs. I'm a little irritated at you right now, not only for that but because you're not cooperating with me. Want to try again? What are Horton's plans?"

The man suddenly realized that he had nothing going for him, and his face drained of color. "Hey. You wouldn't use that whip on me,

would you? I don't know nothin'. No sir, I don't."

The 'breed turned and walked a short distance away. Picking up the whip he said, "I see you want to do this the hard way. I guess I'll give you a little of what Bull gave Theron Cullen."

"Who?" The man's face turned as white as the frosted grass had been the night before. "Who—who's that?" His face twisted and he began struggling with his bonds.

"I'm not the type to fool around," the 'breed said. "I'm going to ask you a question, and you'd better give me the answer I want. Were you with Bull when he whipped Theron Cullen?"

The man's eyes widened as Other Day played with the whip. "Ye—yes!"

"Bull whipped him to death. Did you help?"

"No. I swear to God I didn't."

"Well," the 'breed said, flipping the whip over his shoulder and bringing it forward to crack within an inch of the man's face. The concussion of the tip bloodied his right eye. "What would you do if you were in my position?"

"You—you can't whip me. You can't do the same thing to me. You can't."

Other Day snapped the whip again and brought a branch down from above the man's head. "Why is it that a man like you can beat up people and then expect to be treated like a choir boy when you get caught? A little of the

same medicine for you is in order, I think. Bull will get a big dose if I have anything to say about it."

"Oh, God, no!" the man whimpered. "Don't. I'm sorry. I really am."

Grasping the handle, Other Day threw the whip behind him. "Not good enough. That doesn't bring Theron back. You and Bull made a big mistake leaving Theron's whip behind."

The whip lashed out and caught the man around the chest. His scream was short lived when the whip took another bite a second later. After a few minutes, the man passed out.

Other Day went to the gelding and picked up the man's horse when he found him nearby. Cutting down the unconscious man, he threw him over the saddle, belly down. Swinging onto the bay, Logan picked up the other horse's reins and started south.

After hearing his prisoner confess that it was Horton and Turner who had ordered him to shoot at the camp, Other Day knew that Balland and the L.A. & H. had a case against the other railroad at last.

CHAPTER
TEN

The people of Hades turned to stare at the strange duo riding through their town. Other Day could care less as to what they thought. The man he had captured and whipped north of the end-of-track camp lay across his saddle, hands and feet tied together beneath his horse's belly. The 'breed led the mare through the streets not toward the marshal's office, but toward the small church at the end of the main street. He didn't care what denomination it was. He wanted a minister or a priest to serve as a witness to his delivery of the man he'd caught.

While riding toward the town of Hades, Other Day remembered his first encounter with the L.A. & H. After knocking out Bull Turner,

he'd asked Hold Riggs why they didn't simply call the law in and have him arrested. Riggs had not minced words on the subject. "Won't do no good. As far as we know, we think the marshal for the territory is on the U.L. & B.T.'s side. He'd be outta the pokey before you got him in."

Other Day had never pushed the subject with Riggs, Balland, or anyone else connected with the L.A. & H. The fact that the law didn't seem to be a factor in his acting as troubleshooter had been a plus as far as he was concerned. He didn't care that much for the law, but he wasn't against it either. If a lawman did his job, that was fine with Other Day. It was when they acted like Sheriff Luke Kelp had in Bell's Town, picking and choosing the type of man he wanted to pursue, that Other Day got angry. Apparently the territorial marshal had thrown in with Horton and his men, if what Riggs said was true. Now that he thought on it, Logan wished he had asked Balland about the situation. But he hadn't, and there wasn't time to ride to the camp, ask him, and then head for Hades with his prisoner.

He assumed there was a lawman of some sort in Hades. If it was the territorial marshal, his plan for using the minister or priest would work well. If the law was just a town marshal or town sheriff, the plan would still work.

Other Day reined up in front of the small white church and headed for the house next door, which appeared to be the parsonage.

When he stood on the front step, he raised his hand and knocked on the door.

In seconds, footsteps came toward the front door. When it opened, the half-breed felt taken aback. He'd expected a minister, but instead an attractive young woman confronted him.

"Yes?" she asked, a look of expectancy on her face.

"I—well—that is, is the minister here?"

"Yes, he is. Would you like to step inside while I call him?"

"No, ma'am. I think it'd be better to wait out here so I can keep an eye on my horse and my ah—prisoner."

"Prisoner?" she exclaimed and stood on tiptoe to look past Other Day.

"Yes, ma'am. I would like to speak with the minister. Is he your father?"

"My husband. Just a moment." She turned and disappeared into the house without closing the door.

Other Day peered inside. It was nice and clean and tidy and small, and it was the last element that sent a chill down the 'breed's back. He'd go stark raving mad if he had to live in such a small building.

He turned his attention back to the street and the two horses he'd tied there where he heard footsteps again.

"Yes? I'm the Reverend Robert Knopp. How may I help you?"

Other Day faced the man and said, "My

name's Logan. I'd like you to accompany me to the town's law office to deliver this prisoner."

"Why, for heaven's sake?"

Other Day studied the man for a moment. Tall and on the thin side, the minister had a full head of dark brown hair that appeared to have each hair in its proper place. The 'breed quickly explained how he wanted him to act as a witness without telling him that he suspected the marshal might be less than he appeared.

"Of course I would. Do you suspect your prisoner might be in danger if you hand him over to the law?"

Other Day started for the horses, the minister right behind. "It's something like that, Reverend."

The 'breed opted to walk with the minister and lead the two horses rather than ride. Within minutes, they stood in front of the marshal's office. Other Day noted that Town Marshal was painted on the door. He'd clarify that point once he got inside.

After freeing the captive enough to allow the man to walk, he pushed him up the steps.

"What happened to your back, my dear man?" Reverend Knopp asked.

Before the man could answer, Other Day said quickly, "He fell down a rocky hillside."

Satisfied, Knopp followed the 'breed and his prisoner inside.

Marshal John T. Humprhey stood and stared

at the threesome who entered the office. "Yes? What is it? Whan can I do for you?"

"You the law here?" Other Day asked.

"I am."

"It says town marshal on the sign outside. Are you the territorial marshal?"

"No sir. I'm just what it says—town marshal."

"That's good. I have a prisoner for you." Other Day launched into a brief account of the problems that had confronted the L.A. & H.

"I'll hold him for you, ah, what's your name?"

"Logan," the 'breed said simply. He didn't want to get into a discussion of his first name.

"Right. But I can't guarantee that I can keep him, Mr. Logan."

"How's that?" the 'breed asked, turning to glance at the minister who had an equally puzzled look on his face.

"If the territorial marshal were to come here and demand him, I'd have to give him up. The crime you're accusing him of took place outside Hades and I have no jurisdiction there. The territorial marshal does. He could take him off my hands if he wanted to."

"Of course he doesn't know you got him either, does he?" Other Day said.

The lawman nodded. "That's right."

"Why did you bring me along, Mr. Logan?" Knopp asked.

"I didn't know if this man here was the

territorial marshal or not. I wanted a witness beyond reproach who would swear in a court of law if necessary that I had indeed handed this prisoner over to the lawman here in Hades."

Knopp pursed his lips. "I see."

"That was good thinking on your part, Mr. Logan," the marshal said. "Come on, you." He pushed the prisoner toward the single cell at the back of the room. After he had locked the man up, he turned back to Other Day and said, "How long will he be here?"

"I'll have to have Mr. Balland come in and press charges as soon as it is possible." He turned and walked to the door. "Thank you, gentlemen."

"How's the L.A. & H. doin'?" the marshal asked. "You boys gonna make the deadline?"

"I believe we'll be here on time."

The marshal grinned broadly. "Good. Good."

Outside, Other Day mounted the bay and turned him to ride toward the end-of-track.

"Excellent," Henry Balland exclaimed when Other Day finished telling him about the man he'd captured and taken to the town marshal at Hades.

"I'm no lawyer," Other Day said, "but I feel that since he told me that he worked for Horton and that he was shooting at the camp under Horton's orders and since I saw him doing just that, all of it should make a pretty good case against the U.L. & B.T."

"It does. It does. Up till now we've had no proof of any sort." Balland stopped, a troubled look crossing his face.

"What's the matter, Mr. Balland?" Other Day asked, leaning closer to see better in the coal oil lamplight.

Balland leaned back in his chair. "What about you? If Horton finds out that his man talked to you and that you saw him shooting— Well, it puts you in a very touchy position."

"Don't worry about me. I can take care of myself." Other Day stood to leave.

"I must commend you on the idea of taking the minister with you just in case the marshal was the one in cahoots with the U.L. & B.T."

"The idea struck when I was wondering what sort of people lived in Hades. When I saw the church steeple in the distance, I concluded that a minister who could run a church in a town called Hades had to be either a real honest, hard worker or a man who just didn't give a damn. I thought he would probably fit in the first category."

Balland chuckled and said goodnight.

Other Day slept fitfully the night through, dreaming on occasion of Theron and how he had died. When dawn broke, he opened his eyes, but felt as if he had not slept at all.

The leaden gray sky smelled of snow. A cold wind blew in from the north and west. They had 13 miles of track to lay to reach Hades. The filled-in gorge would be crossed that day if things went smoothly. But the grading was be-

ing held up because of the frozen ground.

Other Day shook his head. It was his problem and it wasn't his problem. He had no idea if the crew could make it to Hades in time or not. He was willing to throw in his lot with theirs and try. That was all any of them could do.

Rolling out of his blankets, he covered them with the tarp and stood up. He started for the kitchen car and a cup of coffee.

Just then, a cry came from the direction of the kitchen car, and he heard the curses of the cook ringing through the early morning air. Then he heard a shot in the distance—someplace far to the north. He wondered what the cook had done. Burned himself? Cut himself?

Just as he reached the table setting outside the car, he saw the cook holding up the coffee pot. Before either Other Day or the cook could say a word, a pan standing on steps leading up to the kitchen car flew up and into the car itself. Off in the distance, another rifle report sounded.

"Ghosts! Goddamn ghosts!" the cook screamed. When he saw Other Day, he held up the coffee pot again and said, "Looky here what them dadburn ghosts went and done."

Other Day stared at the blue-gray pot, twisting back and forth in the man's hand. A hole gaped on either of two sides.

"What caused that?" Other Day asked, a puzzled feeling crossing his mind.

"Danged if'n I know. I was comin' down the steps here when—"

A loud thunk sounded from the side of the railroad car and off in the distance another shot rang out.

"Get down," Other Day yelled, throwing the table over and dropping down behind it.

"What's wrong?" the cook asked along with several other men who were coming to the area for their breakfast.

"Get down. Somebody's shooting at us from a helluva distance."

"What?"

As if to emphasize the 'breed's statement, another thunk sounded and a hole appeared in the table top behind which Other Day hid. The head of one of the men standing near the cook exploded and he collapsed.

The men all dove for protection and the 'breed picked up something from the ground. He turned it over in his hands. A .45 caliber buffalo slug. Horton's men weren't fooling around this time. They probably had sighting scopes of some sort on buffalo guns and were well out of rifle range.

Rolling over and over, Other Day climbed beneath the kitchen car, keeping the table between him and the north at all times, and rolled out the opposite side. Scrambling to his feet, he dashed toward the business car.

He found Henry Balland coming down the steps on the south side, ready to turn the corner and head for breakfast.

"Mr. Balland, wait."

Balland turned and waited for the 'breed.

"Good morning, Other Day."

"They're using .45 caliber buffalo guns this morning. They're a mile or two north of here and've already killed one man. I think they're probably intent on keeping us pinned down all day."

"Good Lord! If that's the case, they'll surely keep us from getting into Hades on time. We only have three days counting today. What can we do?"

"We can do nothing. I'll see what I can do. You keep the men out of sight until I check out the situation." He paused for a moment. "Tell you what, Mr. Balland. Have the men make a few dummies to set around the place—out in the open. It might attract their fire if they see people—or what they think are people—out in the open. Then maybe you and your men won't be in so much danger."

"That's a good idea, Other Day. What are you going to do?"

"I don't know just yet. I have to find them first, then decide how to handle it. While I saddle my horse, can you get me a half-dozen sticks of dynamite and some fuse?"

"Of course," Balland said and set out to fetch the explosives for the 'breed.

Other Day ran crouched over to the tether line and quickly saddled the gelding. When he saw Balland running toward him, he swung into the saddle. He had the train between him and the shooters so he felt safe for the moment despite the high profile he made on horseback.

"Here, Other Day," Balland said, puffing as he came to a stop. "Be careful. How can they be hitting anything from such a distance. I heard one of the men say they were a couple of miles away."

"They're probably using a sighting scope of some sort. If they have the shells loaded with as much powder as possible and are using a shooting tee, they can become pretty accurate if they can read the wind and such just right." Other Day took the half-dozen sticks of dynamite and fuse and put them in his saddle bags. "I'll be back. When you hear one or more explosions from up north, wait a few minutes. If there aren't any more shots, get to work and finish your railroad."

Before Balland could say anything, Other Day turned and drove his heels into the gelding's sides. The animal, sensing the excitement and urgency of his rider, leaped forward and was into a full gallop in seconds. Before the marksmen attacking the camp could fire at him, Other Day rode over the hill and out of sight.

He headed due east for several miles and then turned north. He didn't want the men who were shooting to see him coming. They might be able to keep an eye on him all the time if they chose to use their scopes to do so. Maybe they had field glasses to spy on the camp and him. He didn't know. He'd have to take that chance. If he could get around behind them, he could give them a surprise that would last them

the rest of their lives.

After he had gone several more miles north, he turned and headed back west. If his calculations were close to being right, he should be behind them when he came up to the line of fire on the camp.

Once he had covered a mile or so, the wind, blowing from the west and north, let up for a moment and he heard a shot. Then another. Then a third. A period of quiet followed. Did that mean there were three men? He didn't think a buffalo gun, resting on a shooting tee and being used to shoot at a distance, could be reloaded that fast and be effective.

He studied the terrain to his right. A steady range of hills and bluffs spread to the east and west, offering an obstacle to anyone trying to go farther north in that particular area. He allowed the bay to meander closer to the hill's base to cover him—but from which direction he had no idea.

Three more shots rang out. They were louder this time. Other Day knew he was getting closer, but closer to what? Were the men merely standing out in the open and shooting? They could be doing that since no one from the railroad camp would be able to see them from a distance of one or two miles without glasses. Had they holed up someplace to secrete themselves as much as possible? He'd have to wait and see.

When the next shots rang out, he knew he was close enough to be seen with the naked eye.

He reined to a stop and looked around. From the loudness of the reports, he guessed they couldn't be more than a few hundred yards away from where he stood.

Dropping off the bay, he took the sticks of dynamite and fuse. He slipped the bullwhip over his left shoulder and tied the gelding to a scrub pine tree. Staying close to the hillside and bluffs, he headed west, waiting for the next shots.

They came in a matter of minutes. It seemed that they were coming more frequently now that the day was becoming somewhat brighter. The sun was nowhere in sight, and the sky was still loaded with snow-filled clouds. He felt almost certain it would snow before the day was over. Wondering what that would do to Henry Balland's plans, he continued his way west.

He saw the smoke of the rifles in the next valley and determined that the men were in a cave, but the location of the cave gave him second thoughts.

A bluff, its shear face at least four-hundred-feet high, had several openings in it, and one of them had to be deep enough to hold three men and three buffalo guns on shooting tees. The caves were out of the elements for the most part and virtually impregnable to any counterattack.

He studied the face of the bluff. Although he couldn't see into it, he determined that only one cave was large enough for the men, and he

sighted in on it. How could he possibly get them?

Then Logan saw it. A rope dangled down the side of the bluff. When he followed it with his eyes to the top, he saw that it was tied to a good-sized pine tree. Horton's men had used it to lower themselves and their weapons and supplies to the cave. At first, Other Day had thought there might be another entrance to the cave, but if they had used the rope, then the only way in was the way they had entered.

If it worked for them, it could work for him as well.

After taking in all of the surrounding terrain, he knew he could get to the top of the bluff without being seen by the men in the cave. Returning to the gelding, he mounted and rode east for a short distance, back to a narrow cut he'd seen. Guiding the horse through, he wound his way upward until he came out onto a plateau. Looking westward, he saw three horses tied to a pine tree.

Using the horses as a fixed point he rode across the rocky ground and wound through the shallow ravines and gorges that lay between him and the top of the sheer bluff.

When he was within 100 yards, he dismounted and tied the bay to another scrub tree. He realized there was no sense in letting those other mounts know his gelding was in the area. They might set up enough of a ruckus to have one of the men in the cave come to check things out.

Ten minutes later, he stood at the top and looked down. From there, he could see the muzzles of the three buffalo guns, each weighing 15 pounds, sticking out of the cave. The way they barely moved told him they were using shooting tees to hold the barrels in place. The tree from which the rope hung was six or seven feet to the west of the cave's opening. Looking over the edge again, he decided they could not see the rope from where they were, considering the length of the guns they were using and the fact that the rope itself was flat against the bluff.

Reaching out, he began pulling the rope up in a slow, deliberate manner to avoid making any sort of noise. When the last of the fifty-foot rope lay on top, he untied it and crawled out onto the tree that had held it when the men had lowered themselves to their impregnable position below.

Once he had secured the rope about ten-feet out, he inched his way back in toward the bluff top. Paying out the rope to the east, he lay its full length on the ground. Fixing the center dynamite stick with a short length of fuse, he lay the bundle of six sticks on the ground and tied the rope around his waist. His only concern was that the forthcoming blast might weaken the pine tree to which the rope was tied. To be safe, he decided to try grabbing one of the many outcroppings of rocks on the far side when he reached the end of his rope-controlled flight.

He lit the fuse with a match and pushed out, swinging down in an arc toward the mouth of the cave. When he flew by the cave, he flipped the lighted sticks of dynamite in and disappeared from the view of the men inside.

He heard their shouts and sudden confusion.

"What the hell—?"

"Who was that?"

"What—?"

The blast shot out a column of dirt, rocks, bodies, and buffalo guns as Other Day reached out grasping a rock promontory some ten feet from the top of the bluff. Positioning himself on the rock outcroppings, he pulled his throwing knife and cut the rope from around his waist before moving upward. In seconds, he stood on top of the bluff.

Untying the three horses, he led them back toward the bay and mounted his gelding. Checking out the base of the bluff, he found the three bodies of the men, blown apart, partially buried by the debris that had fallen from the cave.

He smiled grimly. "Rest in pieces, you bastards!"

He rode slowly back toward the camp. When he entered, he found the men hard at work. Henry Balland turned away from Dismus Scott when he saw Other Day riding in leading the three horses.

"I was worried about you, Other Day. Where are the men who were shooting at us?"

"There wasn't enough left of them to bother

with. I thought maybe the camp could use three extra horses." He continued riding toward the tether line and dismounted to tie up the three new mounts.

When he stood next to the bay, he leaned into the horse and put his face against its neck. Bull Turner was not among the men whom he had just killed. A low, ominous growl broke from the half-breed's chest. He was still free, running loose. Sooner or later he'd find Turner and then Theron Cullen's death would be avenged. Other Day clenched his fist until the knuckles cracked.

CHAPTER
ELEVEN

"While Other Day and I talk a bit, I want you to call the men together," Henry Balland said to Dismus Scott, who stood at the rear door of the business car.

"Aye! I'll do it, Mister Balland." He turned and left the car.

Other Day studied Balland. He seemed upset or maybe angry might have been a better way to describe his attitude.

When they were alone, Balland said, "I'm confronting Horton, Other Day. What do you think of that?"

The 'breed frowned. "You mean face to face? One on one? Guns? Knives? Fists? What?"

"Face to face? Yes. But not in a violent way.

I'm going to appeal to his common sense and his sense of fair play. He—"

Other Day turned and walked toward the rear door where he stopped and spun about. "You're funning me, aren't you?"

Balland stared at him. "I'm deadly serious. There's no other way. Good heavens, man! One of our gandy dancers was shot through the head, and another one the guards was wounded by this latest attack of his. Don't you realize that—"

"And you're going to appeal to his common sense? The man who ordered the shootings and the attack on the camp? Do you honestly think he'll sit down and listen to what you have to say? If he would, he'd laugh his head off right before he shot yours off."

Other Day walked toward the desk and sat down in the straightbacked chair opposite his employer. "I don't mean to sound disrespectful toward you, because I admire what you're doing. Men like you are trying to open up the country and help others. You don't understand men like Asa Horton and Bull Turner. They're not much more than animals when it comes to wanting their own way. Before you reach Hades in the next day or so, you're going to see a lot more bloodshed. I only hope it's theirs and not yours and that of your men. I—"

"Why didn't you include yourself in that?" Balland asked. He had a softer look around his eyes, but the anger still clung there.

"I'm used to bleeding. You and your men aren't. I've been shot and cut and beaten up by people over the years. I know how to handle it and the people responsible when they do something like that. You and your men don't. If you confront Horton, you may as well pack up now and start back to Ashton or wherever you came from."

Balland stood. Stroking his chin, he walked around the desk and began pacing up and down the length of the office section. He said nothing and then stopped. He turned and faced the half-breed sitting calmly in front of him. "You honestly think it's a bad idea?"

Other Day nodded.

"It wouldn't work? Even with a show of force by having the entire work crew behind me?"

"Most of all if you took the men. They're not fighters. They're laborers and railroad men. They know how to brawl when they've had too much to drink, but they don't know how to fight to the death or for their lives. Do you want to be responsible for them being gunned down or beaten to a pulp?"

Balland turned and looked out the window of the car toward the distant hills where Other Day had blown the three men to kingdom come with dynamite. "Of course, I don't. What do you propose?"

Just then, the door opened and Dismus Scott entered. "The men are on their way, Mister Balland."

Balland turned to face him. "Tell them—"

"To wait a minute," Other Day said, breaking in.

Balland looked at the troubleshooter. "Ah—yes. Tell them to wait. We'll be finished in a moment."

Scott nodded and left the car.

"Why have them wait? If they're not to be involved, why have them wait?" Balland fixed his full attention on Other Day.

"Why have them think you chewed some locoweed, calling them together and then telling them to leave without talking to them. You'll have to say something, but say something that's right."

"Of course, you're right. Going back to what we were talking about—do you have a plan?"

"I have a plan but I don't think I should tell you what it is."

Balland stared at him. "Since I'm your employer, I think it might be wise if you did."

"You hired me to be your troubleshooter, didn't you?"

"I did."

"Let's say I'm going to do my job and shoot some trouble."

"My God, man. You can't take Horton and his men on by yourself."

"I tell you what, Mr. Balland: you build the railroad since you know how, and I'll take care of Horton. I know how to do that."

Balland stormed behind his desk and slapped

his open hand down. The smacking sound brought Melanie to the office from the compartment where she slept.

"What is it, Father?" She looked at her father and then fixed her attention on Other Day.

"This young fool wants to take on Horton's gang by himself while we finish the road. It's out-and-out suicide." Balland didn't tear his eyes from the 'breed.

Other Day stared back, an air of confidence about him. "Do you have any idea as to how many men Horton has working for him?"

Balland frowned. "Of course not. How could I?"

"He had around fifteen or twenty that I could calculate. He's got four less now since one is in jail and three are spread around the countryside up north. So now he has between eleven or sixteen men left. If anything, I'd say the odds were against them."

Balland's jaw dropped. "How can you say that?"

"They've got me angry and I'm going to get them. Every last one of them."

A heavy silence filled the car, and a look of acceptance replaced the one of frustration on Balland's face. "Very well, do what you must."

The superintendent walked to the rear of the car and out onto the platform to deliver a pep talk of sorts to the gathered workers.

Other Day stood and followed him to stand behind Balland while he talked. Melanie, a

perplexed look of admiration and fear mixed on her face, stared after the 'breed and then followed him meekly to the platform.

"Men," Balland began and was immediately cut off by the sound of gunshots coming from the west.

Other Day reacted immediately. Leaping into the saddle of the bay gelding loosely tied to the rear platform, he shouted. "Those shots came from the direction of the grading-work site. Follow me there."

He spurred the gelding and was galloping toward the end of the work camp in seconds. The shots continued for a few moments and then stopped abruptly. Other Day rode at a full gallop and, when he knew he was almost in sight of the grading crew, reared back on the reins. The bay slid on his hind legs and reared after Other Day leaped from the saddle. Smacking the horse on his hindquarters, the bay trotted off to the east.

Other Day threw himself on the ground and inched his way forward. When he could look over the crest of the small hill, he saw the work site. Men lay everywhere. He didn't move. He didn't know if the killers were still about. Waiting for several moments, he pushed himself up and waited more. Nothing happened and he stood up.

After running the 50 yards toward the bodies of the men, he found them dead of gunshot wounds. Even the two teams of mules had been

slaughtered by the killers.

A moan brought him around and he found Hold Riggs, turning over. Blood flowed from his chest and gory spittle trickled from his mouth. Other Day dropped to his knees and picked the wounded man up, gently cradling him in his arms across his legs.

"Did you see any of their faces, Riggs?"

Riggs barely nodded. "Ye—yes."

"Were they Horton's men?"

Again he managed to nod, but couldn't speak.

"Was Bull Turner with them?"

Riggs coughed and spit up blood for several long seconds before he stopped. Then he nodded and whispered weakly. "He—he led—them. He shot me."

Riggs' head lolled to the side and Other Day knew he was dead. Standing, after carefully laying the dead man on the earth, the 'breed counted the men. Sixteen bodies and four mules. He felt his anger growing. This was senseless slaughter to prove a senseless point. Horton wanted the bond money the people of Hades had voted on to give to the first railroad company to bring a train to that town. He didn't want to compete on a fair basis by building a road. All he wanted to do was prevent Balland and his company from reaching Hades. Then he and his men would take over their work and pick up the $100,000 grant. Counting Theron and the man who had his head blown off by a .45 caliber slug, there

were 18 dead men from the L.A. & H. There had been only three fatalities on the U.L. & B.T.'s side, and they had more or less asked for it. The men who had been gunned down that morning were just doing their job. They weren't gun-fighters, like the three he'd blown to pieces the day before.

His thoughts were broken up when Balland, Scott, and a handful of men from the track-laying crew rode up. Melanie arrived a few minutes later in a buckboard.

Balland looked at the dead men, tears running down his face. "Oh, my good God. They're dead. All of them are dead." He looked to the 'breed for confirmation.

Other Day nodded.

"That's it then. I'm finished. Completely washed up. Without the grading crew, we can't lay track. Even if we could put together a crew from the men we have, it would cut the track-laying crew by that many more men. No. It's all over. The Lorraine, Ashton and Hades is dead."

"I know it doesn't look good for you, Mister Balland," the 'breed said. "Maybe I can track down whoever did it. Maybe Hades will give you an extension if you can prove the U.L. & B.T. people killed these men."

"You don't understand, Other Day. The bond issue is governed by law. Even if they wanted to extend the time, they couldn't because the bond issue is like a law. It can be repealed but

it can't be tinkered with in the way you're suggesting. Even if they did, with our work force cut down like it is, it would take too long. Besides, it's getting close to snowing, and when that happens we may as well forget it. It's ironic but true. Everything is against us. The ground is hard as rock. We'd have to blast every cubic foot of earth needed to grade the roadbed. It's—"

"What you just said about the ground being as hard as rock, Mister Balland," Other Day said, "gives me an idea. I don't know if it'll work or not. But Mister Scott would know, I'll bet. Why not lay the track on the bare ground? Get your rails into Hades along with the train and then come back and finish the grading later."

He turned to Dismus Scott and then to Henry Balland. Scott's face reacted first. "It would work. *Hoot mon!* It would work."

Balland turned to the engineer. "Are you sure, Scott?"

"Aye, Mister Balland, sir. It would work."

"Then what are we waiting for? Get going." Balland turned to Other Day. "By rights, I should suggest to the board of directors that they make you the president of the road. I don't know how I can ever thank you. If we get into Hades on time, it'll be because of you and no one else."

"What about these dead men?" Other Day asked, a somber look on his face.

"I'll appoint a burial crew and get on it right away. What are you going to do?"

"I'm going after Bull Turner."

"Wouldn't it be better to have you here in case they come back? I know I'd feel better if you were here."

"So would I," Melanie said, stepping closer to her father and looking at the 'breed, an expression of worry and concern on her face.

"Right now their guard will be down because they think they've dealt you a finishing blow. They think you need the grading crew to get into Hades. While they're patting themselves on the back about their good job, I'll be hunting them down and be able to take them off guard."

Balland frowned for a moment. "I won't argue with you. All I'll say is be careful."

"Be very careful," Melanie added.

Other Day didn't acknowledge their admonition. Instead he turned and walked toward the scene of the shootings. He studied the ground and picked out the differences in the hoof marks. The bastards had ridden right in on them, taking the crew off guard and shooting them down where they stood.

He walked around for several more minutes, following the paths that the different horses had taken. There had been nine of them. Nine murderers. Nine bastards who were going to be hunted down like the animals they were.

He'd show them no mercy. The one he really wanted was Bull Turner. Turner had to be some sort of killing beast as far as Other Day was determined. Sure Other Day had killed men in his time. Too many. And the one thing he feared more than anything was that his reputation would start moving ahead of him. That he didn't want. He'd wiped out Half Ear Hantelmann's gang and Ike Eurlong's gang single-handedly. He'd lost count of how many men had been involved. But the gangs had stood between him and the men he actually wanted—Half Ear Hantelmann for raping and murdering his mother, and Ike Eurlong for having done the same horrendous crimes to Belle Doolin, the one woman Other Day thought he could have loved.

Bull Turner was something else of a problem to him. Bull was like an animal. He didn't seem to care the slightest bit for anyone. He'd hired out to the highest bidder to perform his murderous acts. He'd whipped Theron Cullen to death. Theron was a good man and one Other Day had liked as a friend, which was a rare occurence in itself.

After fetching his bay, he mounted the animal and rode off south as Bull and his men had. Walking the gelding, he kept his attention to the ground following the nine animals' tracks. Eight miles to the south of the grading site, he found the tracks veering sharply to the right and toward a cut in a singular row of hills

that he had paralleled for the last hour or so.

Deciding that the gang might be near by, Other Day elected to leave the gelding in a dense grove of trees and go ahead on foot toward the small valley-like cut. He slipped the Winchester from its boot and checked its magazine. It was full. While he walked, he continued thinking on Bull Turner and the man who had hired him, Asa Horton. He'd never laid eyes on Horton, but he had heard him the night he and Theron had stolen Horton's dynamite when Horton had come into the storage building in back of the Gilded Garter.

The 'breed's body began tingling, and he knew he was drawing closer to Bull and his gang. Slipping through the trees that covered most of the opening was no problem, and when he was inside the box-like valley that opened before him, he could see the tether line of the gang's mounts. He hid behind a pine tree when he saw movement.

A man walked to the tether and saddled a horse. That meant he was going somewhere and the only way out of the valley was past the spot where Other Day had positioned himself. Without waiting, he leaped up, grabbing a low hanging branch, and swung himself into the pine tree. Standing up on a branch, he placed his body on line with the trunk and waited. In minutes, the rider galloped by and headed his mount southeast.

Other Day watched. The only thing that lay in that direction was Ball Town. Looking up at the gray sky he wondered where the sun was exactly, but guessed he had about four hours of daylight left. Once darkness set in, he'd leave the perch and stalk the killer animals in the valley.

When darkness did come, it blackened the entire countryside. No moon, no stars, no relief of any sort from nature itself. The only light for miles around was the glow of the campfire Bull and his men had lighted.

Other Day checked his .44 and patted the three knives he had secreted on himself. The last thing he checked was Theron's whip—his whip. He was ready. Just as he was about to drop from his tree branch, he saw a shadow cross in front of the glow of the campfire. He waited. The shadow turned out to be a man walking toward the opening where Other Day had positioned himself. Probably the men had decided to post a guard or maybe to keep watch for the man who had ridden to Ball Town. It would be easy to ride by a hidden opening like the mouth of the box valley on a black night such as the one that gripped the countryside.

The man passed within ten feet of the tree in which the 'breed waited and took up a post about 50 feet to the east, practically in the

opening itself. Before the man sat down, Other Day dropped from the tree without a sound. He could barely make out the man in the gloom and decided against the throwing knife. He'd have to stalk the guard or run the risk of a rear attack.

Keeping trees and bushes between him and the fire so his silhouette wouldn't be noticeable, he inched his way toward the sentry. The man sat with his back to a pine-tree trunk and gazed across the expanse of dark open countryside. Other Day moved to the opposite side of the tree against which the man rested without making a sound. Eyeing the tree trunk, he estimated it to be no more than two feet across. He reached down and slipped the Bowie knife out of its scabbard with his right hand. Crouching down, he leaned to one side and saw where the man's head rested. Then with one swift motion, the razor-sharp knife swept through the dark night, slitting open the man's throat. The only sound the man made was a brief gurgling before pitching forward.

The 'breed stepped around the tree and wiped the blade off on the man's shirt. Slipping it back in its sheath, he turned and faced the fire. Bull Turner and the rest of Horton's men were next.

He passed through the intervening distance like a ghost, making no noise, barely visible as he used the brush and trees to his advantage. When he was within earshot, he stopped

moving and listened. He gripped his knife when he realized he heard Bull Turner talking.

"We're waiting here. We're waiting for orders from Mister Horton. Orders is orders, my fine fellows, and we'll obey them. Do you understand?"

"I only thought it would be nice if we could get some whiskey, Bull. That's all I meant."

"Well, whiskey is not an order tonight. Knocking out that railroad is. Mister Horton said we should wait here after we finished the grading crew and he'd come himself to tell us first-hand what we are to do next. By gawd, we've got 'em on the run this time."

"You don't think we should have waited to make sure they was done?" another man asked.

"You don't believe in obeying orders do you, my fine fellow. We're doing what we was told to do. And by gawd, we'll do just that. Understand?"

Other Day heard the man mumble an agreement and moved a bit closer. He wondered if they'd sleep that night or if they were to wait for Horton because he'd show up before dawn. From where he was now, he could count the men in camp and found that there were seven. One had gone to Ball Town and Logan had already dispatched one.

What he wanted was a more spread-out

group. If they were on their own, he could stalk them better. He had to scatter them. Raising the Winchester, he squeezed off three fast rounds. Three men went down, two pitched into the fire and the third splayed out on his backside dead.

Bull and the other men stood unable to move for a split second. Then the remaining four dashed into the dark, drawing their handguns. All four returned shots at the area where the rifle shots had come from but hit nothing. The 'breed had already circled to the right to come up behind them and found a man crouched behind a bush, peering into the darkness on the other side of the campfire.

Other Day drew his throwing knife and, in one motion, sent the whirling missive of death on its way. The man's muscles reacted, and he stiffened as the ten-inch blade pierced his heart from the backside. He struggled to stand for a second, then fell forward into the brush.

"Wes? What happened? Is that you over there?" a voice called out.

Other Day wished it had been Bull. He'd like to know where that man was out here in the dark. Instead of looking for Bull, he turned his attention on the man who had called out. Passing the body of his victim, he reached out and pulled the throwing knife from his back, and quickly cleaned it on the dead man's shirt. Just as he was about to move on, he heard a

branch crack in front of him.

Other Day reacted instantly and threw his knife as soon as he saw the form of a man looming over him. "Who—?" was all the man managed to say before the knife punctured his throat. He gurgled and struggled to breathe but nothing happened, and he pitched forward, almost knocking over Other Day.

Once more Logan claimed the knife and cleaned it before slipping it back into the sheath that hung down inside of his shirt in back.

"I got 'im, Bull," a voice cried out 15 feet to the 'breed's left.

Other Day heard a gun being cocked and he threw himself to the left, drawing his .44 in the same motion. Before the other man could squeeze off a shot, the Colt in the 'breed's hand barked once. A bloodcurdling scream told him that he'd found the man.

He and Bull were alone.

"Bull?"

"Who are you? Where are you?"

"You know who it is, Bull. We've met a couple of times. Once at the grading site and once at the Gilded Garter."

"The half-breed? Well, my fine fellow, you've gone out of your way to find me, haven't you? Hasn't he, boys?"

"Who are you talking to, Bull? You're the only one left and you're next."

"Boys? Wes? Benny? Bob? Grant?"

"They're all dead, Bull, and you're next."

"Why'd you do that? What'd you have agin my boys and me?" His voice almost whined the words.

"You cracked my ribs for one thing."

"Ah, I was just funnin'. Can't you take a little funnin', half-breed?"

"You also killed a friend of mine. You whipped him to death. Was that fun, too?"

Bull didn't answer for several minutes. Then he said, "Why don't you come out and fight fair like a man, half-breed? Shootin' men in the back ain't my way of fightin'."

Other Day listened carefully. His enemy had moved to the right. He was trying to sneak up on the 'breed. Other Day moved off into the dark away from the fire and came up behind the spot from where he'd heard Bull call.

"Hey, Bull?" the 'breed called and then quickly moved off ten feet to the left without making a sound.

A shot rang out and struck the area from where Other Day had called.

"You still alive, half-breed?" Bull asked, a sneer sounding in his voice.

"Is whipping a man to death when he's tied up your idea of fighting fair?" Other Day moved again, closer to where Bull hid.

Another shot rang out and struck the ground where the 'breed had been standing.

"I'm ready to fight you, Bull. You ready to fight me?"

"I'm ready, half-breed."

"Come on out, Bull."

"Here I come, you half-breed heathen."

CHAPTER
TWELVE

"How we gonna do this, half-breed?" Bull yelled after several minutes passed.

"How do you mean?" Other Day answered and moved off to his right.

"I don't trust you and you don't trust me. How we gonna know the other fellow's unarmed?"

"Good question, Bull. Tell you what. Take off your shirt and throw it into the clearing by the fire. I'll do the same. Then you throw your gun and I'll do the same. Sound fair?"

Bull didn't answer right away and then called out. "It sounds fair to me. You wouldn't lie to me, would you, half-breed?"

"Perish the thought."

"What about your rifle, half-breed?"

Other Day smiled grimly. The bastard would have to remember the Winchester. "I'll throw it out first." Other Day heaved the rifle out toward the fire after emptying the magazine.

"You're dead serious about fightin' me, ain't you? Never let it be said that Bull Turner denied anyone the opportunity to get his brains kicked out. Here's my shirt."

Other Day watched the gray flannel shirt float out from behind a bush. He stripped his own off and concealed the throwing knife and its sheath behind a pile of rocks. Then, he threw his shirt out. "Here's mine, Bull."

"Here's my six-gun."

Other Day watched the piece rotate as it flew through the air to land near his rifle. He emptied his .44 and threw it out next. "That should do it, Bull. You're without your six-gun and so am I. We're without shirts, so we can't have a concealed weapon," Other Day said, reaching down to pat the Bowie knife in his right boot. "I've thrown my rifle out and I think maybe you should too, Bull. Throw it out—now."

"You don't miss a trick, do you, half-breed?"

"I try not to," the 'breed said and watched a rifle sail out from behind the scrub pines where Bull had moved.

"I'm comin' out now, half-breed. Come on and I'll give you a lesson in fightin'."

Other Day caught sight of some movement and the bulk of a man stepped out. Bull Turner

stood six feet six inches and weighed in the neighborhood of 300 pounds. His belly hung over his belt but the muscles in his arms and shoulders bespoke monstrous strength. The 'breed gripped the handle of the whip and stuck it in the back of his pants, letting the whip trail out behind him. He wanted to be able to approach Bull straight on so he wouldn't immediately see the whip.

He took a step toward the fire and Bull turned to face him. "You're a lot smaller than I remember, half-breed. Why you want to die this way?"

"Let's not talk about that yet, Bull. I want to settle a score for Theron Cullen first."

"Who the hell's that?" He screwed his massive face up into forced thought and stared at the 'breed.

"The man you whipped to death while he hung from a tree. Remember?"

"Oh, him. Did he die? I'm sorry to hear that. I didn't think I'd whipped him enough to do that. And you want to settle the score for that?"

"You bet I do." Other Day said and reached behind his back, grabbing the handle of the bullwhip. He snapped it forward and caught Bull off guard. Bull yelped in pain when the popper hit him in the chest.

"Yeouch! You sonofabitch! You got a whip. That ain't fair. You said," he stopped and tried to duck the whip again, but the tip found his belly this time. "Goddamn! You ain't fightin'

fair."

"So I lied!" Other Day said and brought the whip into play again. This time he snapped the popper at the man's face and sliced his nose off. Blood spurted out from the wound, and Bull stood dumbfounded at the peculiar turn of events. He brought his hands up to protect his face, but not before the tip flashed again through the firelight to snap at his right eye. His screams punctuated the rifle-like crack of the whip.

His vision reduced to half, Bull turned to run, and Other Day was right on his trail, slashing after him with the whip. Chunks of skin and flesh flew from Bull's back as the 'breed played the popper to do the work instead of lashing him the way Bull had done to Theron.

"Stop right there, Bull," Other Day said and the huge man obeyed.

"Enough, enough! You goddamn savage! You heathen! Stop it!"

Other Day reared back and snapped the whip, taking the other eye. "I will just as soon as you learn that you're whipped and stop calling me names."

"I'm blind. I'm blind. I can't see." Bull whimpered, covering his bleeding eyes with both hands.

"Bull Turner? You here?" A voice called out from the direction of the valley entrance.

"You make one sound, Bull, and you'll be worse off than my gelding," Other Day

whispered.

Bull continued crying and sobbing but said nothing.

Other Day circled back toward the fire and drew the Bowie knife as he went. A well-dressed man and a gunslinger walked into the glow of the fire.

"I don't like this, Mr. Horton," the gunslinger said and slowly drew his gun, his eyes sweeping over the darkness that surrounded the campsite.

Other Day stood up on the man's left and snaked the whip out toward him. The tip wrapped around the barrel of the gun, and Logan yanked it out of the man's grasp before he knew anyone else was around.

"Just stand right there," Other Day said quietly, "and don't make a sound. Both of you lie down on your bellies."

"Who are you?" Horton asked.

"Other Day Logan. Troubleshooter for the L.A. & H. Mr. Balland wants to press some charges against you and your men, Mister Horton. I'm in a rather bad mood and I'd suggest that you do everything I say or you might be sorry—real sorry."

The sun had barely broken over the eastern horizon, but the camp was already up and getting ready for the final push into Hades when Other Day rode into camp leading his strange pack train. Three horses trailed in

behind him as he led them toward the business car of the L.A. & H. Each horse had a man draped across the saddle.

Henry Balland stepped out onto the rear platform and stopped, his eyes widening as he watched Other Day dismount. The 'breed walked over to the other horses and, one by one, tipped each man off by the head so he landed on his feet.

"Mister Balland, I'd like to introduce Mister Asa Horton to you along with some shypoke who chose the wrong side and one Bull Turner who won't be bothering too many people any more."

Bull stood fighting to keep his balance without his sight. He whimpered from the pain of his wounds.

"Shut up, you big mule," Horton growled.

Bull began crying.

"No wonder nothing went right for me," Horton snapped. "Look at the men I hired."

"Mister Balland, I believe today is the day the train is supposed to arrive in Hades, or is my calculation wrong?" Other Day asked, his face immobile.

"That it is, Other Day. We have only four miles to go. The track being laid without grading is working beautifully, and we'll begin grading and ballasting as soon as we reach Hades. What do you propose doing with your prisoners?"

"I want to talk to you about that," Other Day

said, climbing up onto the rear platform. He turned and looked at Dismus Scott. "Can you put our guests there in a boxcar and post four fully armed guards to watch over them. If anyone of them tries to do anything other than scratch, shoot him. Understand?"

"Aye. I do. I do." Scott turned to do as he had been bid, and Other Day followed Henry Balland into the business car.

The ringing of the last few spikes being driven home echoed through the town of Hades. When it stopped a moment of silence followed, and then a cheer erupted from the townspeople and the railroad workers alike. The Lorraine, Ashton and Hades had met the time limit and the bond money belonged to that railroad.

The work train backed up to a point half a mile out of town and waited for the townspeople who wanted to brag to their children and friends that they had been on board the first train into Hades to come out and climb on. The throng swept over the countryside toward the work train, and when as many people were on board as could be accommodated, the locomotive blew its whistle.

Other Day beamed at the engineer. "Could I blow it?"

"I don't see no reason you shouldn't."

Other Day reached up and grabbed the rope and pulled. The ensuing shriek pierced the air

for almost a minute.

"Hey, you'll use up all my steam and we never will get the train into Hades." The engineer laughed and looked over at his fireman. "Well, Burgy, load her up, 'cause I think we'll be runnin' into and outta Hades the rest of the day."

The fireman nodded and opened the firebox doors. He shoveled in several scoops of coal and closed the doors to the fire.

The fourth man in the cab, Henry Balland, smiled broadly at Other Day. "We should probably name a station or town after you. I don't think this would have been finished if it hadn't been for you. Of course I don't agree with what you did to the one man, Turner, but I won't fault you for it either."

"I feel that Theron will be happy now, no matter where he's hunting at now, Mr. Balland."

"Your idea for Horton was most apropos."

"I don't know what that means, but if you think making him pay to ride on the L.A. & H. to go to Hades and be arrested fit the situation, then I guess it's all right."

The train whistled again and the locomotive lurched ahead. A cry and shout went up from the passengers hanging onto the flat cars, the ballast gondolas, and the box cars when the train moved toward Hades.

Perched on the front flat car with Dismus Scott and six other men holding rifles on their

prisoners, Asa Horton frowned and cursed at everyone and everything as the train neared Hades.

A sign, which Other Day had printed, hung from his neck and stated: "I am the first paying customer on the L.A. & H. It is a much better railroad than the U.L. & B.T., which I own."

Other Day's bay gelding paced alongside the slow-moving train, his reins tied to the grab iron of the tender, next to the cab. Just as the train reached the stopping place at the site of the future passenger station, Other Day grabbed Henry Balland's hand.

"Congratulations and thank you for the job," he said, shaking the superintendent's hand.

"I wish you wouldn't leave now, Other Day. I could use you for other projects that are coming my way now that this one is completed."

"I've overstayed now. I'm heading back down south where it doesn't get so cold. Say goodbye to Melanie for me."

"I think she might be unhappy that you're leaving without telling her yourself."

"You know better than that. I'm doing both her and you a favor by leaving now." Other Day forced himself to smile.

"Perhaps you're right. Goodbye, Other Day Logan. You're one helluva man."

Other Day turned and swung down into the saddle of the bay. He touched the brim of his

Stetson in salute and turned the horse's head away from the train.

Nudging the horse in the sides, the rider headed south.

Get more bang for your money with special, expanded and double editions of the hottest Adult Western in town...

More action, more adventure, more shady ladies!

BUCKSKIN DOUBLE EDITION: HANGFIRE HILL/CROSSFIRE COUNTRY by Roy LeBeau.
In *Hangfire Hill*, Morgan faces a deadly showdown with a wealthy mine owner's hired guns before he can stake his claim on the Golden Penny Mine. In *Crossfire Country*, he tracks down the killers of a Canadian land baron with the help of a willing Ojibway squaw. Two complete westerns in one volume.

_____2701-1 $3.95

BUCKSKIN SPECIAL EDITION: THE BUCKSKIN BREED by Kit Dalton
This giant volume is the bawdy, blazing story of the Buckskin breed, a passel of children sired by Morgan's father, Buckskin Frank Leslie. Morgan had his back to the wall, put there by a family he had never known. It was brother against brother and the winner would walk away with his life.

_____2587-6 $3.95US/$4.95CAN

LEISURE BOOKS
ATTN: Customer Service Dept.
276 5th Avenue, New York, NY 10001

Please send me the book(s) checked above. I have enclosed $ _____
Add $1.25 for shipping and handling for the first book; $ .30 for each book thereafter. No cash, stamps, or C.O.D.s. All orders shipped within 6 weeks. Canadian orders please add $1.00 extra postage.

Name _____

Address _____

City _____ State _____ Zip _____
Canadian orders must be paid in U.S. dollars payable through a New York banking facility.   ☐ Please send a free catalogue.